BURN SO BAD

Into The Fire Series

J.H. CROIX

J.H. CROIX

This is a work of fiction. Names, characters, businesses, places, events and incidents are either the products of the author's imagination or used in a fictitious manner. Any resemblance to actual persons, living or dead, or actual events is purely coincidental.

Copyright © 2018 J.H. Croix

Cover design by Cormar Covers

 Created with Vellum

To DBC - you are my antidote to the pitfalls of life, and you never fail to make me laugh. Plus, you love our dogs like crazy, and that means everything.

Sign up for my newsletter for information on new releases & get a FREE copy of one of my books!

http://jhcroixauthor.com/subscribe/

Follow me!
jhcroix@jhcroix.com
https://amazon.com/author/jhcroix
https://www.bookbub.com/authors/j-h-croix
https://www.facebook.com/jhcroix

BURN SO BAD

Levi

Where there's smoke there's fire, and hate
can always turn into love.
Lucy hates me. She especially hates how
much I want her.
And sweet h*ll do I want her.
But she can't be bothered to even give me the
time of day.
I should give up the chase, but I can't.
It's more than a spark between us. It's a
bonfire.
Fate rolls the dice and lands Lucy right where
I want her.
She needs my help, and I need her.

One taste, and I'm lost. I'll do anything to have her and to hold her.
To make her mine.

Lucy

Levi drives me crazy, and not the good kind of crazy.
He's smoldering hot and so handsome, it's downright dangerous.
A hotshot firefighter, he nearly sets me on fire whenever he's around.
Perhaps it's an occupational hazard.
He teases me every chance he gets and tempts me to let down my guard.
I definitely don't need a man. But Levi's more than a man. He's a man on octane fuel—pure masculinity practically oozes from his pores.
One night of weakness, and I tumble into his fire.
It's more than desire. It's how I feel when I'm with him—safe and protected. I never want to let go.

Chapter One

LEVI

"Where's Lucy?" I asked.

Amelia Masters sighed. "I just told you. Up..."

Her words were cut off by another voice.

"Oh for God's sake, I'm stuck up here."

I glanced up to see a flash of bright blonde hair just past the corner of the roof.

"Lucy's up there?" Cade Masters asked over my shoulder as he approached us.

"Yes! I'm up here. How hard is this to figure out?" Lucy called from above.

I looked back to Amelia. Lucy Caldwell was her best friend, and they owned and ran Kick A** Construction together. We were at one of their current job sites where they were building a new home.

Cade and I were hotshot firefighters in Willow Brook, Alaska and had volunteered to help when Amelia, Cade's wife, called. It was clear why she'd called Cade directly, rather than the main dispatch number. Lucy sounded pissed. Knowing Lucy the way I did, I'd bet she was beyond annoyed she needed help. She most definitely wouldn't have appreciated an entire crew showing up to handle this.

"Care to explain," Cade said dryly.

"We were working on getting the roof beams in place for the cathedral ceiling. Lucy got trapped up there when one of the beams fell and broke the ladder in half." Amelia paused, her gaze concerned. "I'm guessing she got hurt too because the beam whacked a two-by-four on its way down, and it flipped and hit her. You know Lucy though, she told me to shut up and stop worrying."

"Ah, so that's why you told us to bring a ladder," Cade said, his gaze clearing.

"Yeah, why'd you bring the cherry picker?" she asked in return, glancing over to our vehicle.

Cade and I had collectively decided it would be better to drive the large truck with its extendable arm and bucket if we needed it.

"In case Lucy was hurt," I interjected. "We figured it was better to have this than to try to carry her down a ladder. All you told us was Lucy needed help getting off the scaffolding."

"What the hell are you guys talking about?" Lucy hollered from her perch.

I walked around the corner of the partially constructed home and glanced up. Lucy was perched atop some scaffolding, her blonde hair standing out against the blue sky above.

"How ya doin?" I called.

"I'll be better when one of you gets me down," Lucy replied.

Even from two stories above, she managed to convey her prickly, get-the-hell-away-from-me attitude. From my vantage point, I could see her cradling her arm. I doubted she'd fess up to being injured, so I didn't comment on it. A thread of worry wove through me. I didn't like thinking about her being in pain. Not one bit.

"We'll be up there in just a few," I called up.

I walked back toward Cade. "Let's do this. Better to use the bucket than a ladder."

In short order, Cade was easing me upward in the bucket. Inside of another minute, I was level with where Lucy was.

The moment she saw me, her eyes narrowed and her lips tightened. That bit about Lucy not enjoying anyone's help? Well, she was *not* pleased.

Even with her blond hair a windblown mess, her skin flushed and smudged with dirt, and wearing heavy-duty jeans and a loose t-shirt, she was flat out gorgeous.

"Hey Lucy," I said, my eyes going to her arm.

She'd seated herself on the boards across the top of the scaffolding and slowly straightened, flinching slightly when her arm bumped against one of the metal bars on the scaffolding.

"Your arm okay?" I asked.

Lucy's wide blue eyes swung to me. 'It's fine," she snapped.

I bit back a retort. Normally, I loved to tease Lucy. In fact, the crankier she got, the more I reveled in amping her up. A bit ago, I'd tried to get her to go out with me, but she wouldn't even deign to have dinner with me, so I'd dropped it. That didn't change the fact I wanted her. But I didn't think about that now. Not the time or place. It was quite obvious she was in pain. She could be as cranky as she wanted. I just wanted to get her out of here safely and get her arm taken care of.

"Bring me a little closer," I called down to Cade, eyeing the boards under Lucy's feet and assessing whether it was best for me to lift her from here, or climb out.

Cade carefully adjusted the bucket, bringing it flush against the edge of the scaffolding.

"Perfect," I called to him.

I looked over at Lucy. "How about…"

She stepped to the side of the bucket and started to climb in herself.

"Hey, slow down," I said quickly. "Let me…"

The second I spoke, she lost her balance and reflexively reached to grab the scaffolding with her injured arm. She cried out and lurched, tumbling off the side of the scaffolding. In a flash, I caught her by her other arm.

For a few seconds, the nearly impenetrable get-the-hell-away-from-me expression fell from her face. Her sky blue eyes were wide with fear. I might've been calm—because staying calm in the midst of any kind of emergency was what years of training and working as a hotshot firefighter had taught me—but my heart clenched and worry roared through me.

"I've got you Lucy," I said calmly.

I did. I had a firm grip on her arm. She didn't weigh much. At all. Her attitude belied her size. She was quiet, her eyes locked to my face, before she nodded sharply.

Holding Lucy's gaze, I adjusted my stance and slowly leaned over, hooking my other hand under her armpit. I lifted her up and into the bucket in one swift move. I cradled her against me when I drew her all the way over the side. Once I knew she was safe, I took a slow breath and glanced to her.

"You okay?"

Her eyes flicked away, and she looked at the scaffolding and back to me.

"I guess I should thank you," she said, only the slightest hint of begrudging in her tone.

Leave it to Lucy to be annoyed I'd saved her from falling two stories and possibly killing herself in the process.

"No need to thank me. It's my job," I replied with a wink.

Her eyes narrowed. I didn't know what it was about her, but damn she got to me. It didn't matter that she'd just had a pretty serious brush with danger. Now that her safety was certain, I couldn't help but try to tease her. She kicked her legs, her feet bumping against my thigh.

"Okay, you can put me down now. Consider me rescued," she said with a little laugh.

I hesitated. This was the closest I'd ever gotten to her, and I didn't want to give it up just yet. She thumped her feet against my thigh again.

"Seriously Levi, you can put me down," she insisted, her tone flustered.

I reluctantly eased her down, taking care not to jostle her arm that was quite obviously injured whether she'd admit it or not. Once she was on her feet, I looked over at her as I stepped back.

"No sense in lying. How's your arm?" I asked.

Amelia called up at that moment. "Is Lucy okay?

Lucy sighed and rolled her eyes. "Oh my God. I can talk, you know. I'm fine!"

"Well, don't get all pissy with me," Amelia retorted. "You almost fell from up there. We get to be worried."

I leaned over the side. "She's safe and sound," I called, giving Amelia a thumbs up. "Cade, you wanna bring this thing down now?"

I looked back to Lucy. The bucket jostled slightly as Cade started to lower us.

"So? Your arm?"

She met my eyes with an elaborate sigh. "I think I might've broken it."

For a moment, I forgot this was Lucy, the living, breathing definition of touchy. I stepped to her side and slid my hands down her upper arm, carefully unfolding it. I was moving on reflex. As a hotshot firefighter, I was trained to handle anything and everything, including medical emergencies from minor to major. As my touch traveled along her forearm, I didn't feel a break, but it was already swelling. She was so petite. She barely reached my chin. I could wrap one hand around her wrist with room to spare.

"I'm not feeling a break, but it could be just a crack, or bad bruising. It's swelling along your radius here," I murmured, keeping my touch light as I brushed across the area.

When I glanced up, her gorgeous blue eyes were inches away. My gaze coasted over her face, taking in her fine-boned features—the slight tilt of her nose, her high cheekbones, the delicate arch of her brow, and her full, perfectly bow-shaped pink lips, complete with a dimple in the center of her bottom lip. A streak of dirt on her cheek was endearing, if only because it was so out of place on her face.

My gaze landed on the rapid flutter of her pulse in her neck. My cock twitched, my body tightening in response.

I whipped my eyes back up. This was definitely not the time or place for me to be getting hot over Lucy.

I expected her to shove me away, not that there was much space if she did. Yet, she didn't.

Her mouth twisted with a sigh. "Well, whatever happened, it hurts."

I'd completely lost track of what I'd said for a moment. The feel of her arm resting in my hands nudged me back on track.

"Amelia mentioned she thought a two-by-four hit you."

Lucy nodded. "Yeah, the beam fell and hit the two-by-four on the way down. It whacked me good when it flipped over."

She gave her arm a little tug. "Can I have my arm back?"

I reluctantly let go. Up to these last few moments, Lucy had been a challenge I wanted to beat. Always quick to argue, always turning me down, rarely smiling...and beautiful, so fucking beautiful, she took my breath away.

Conveniently, or not, depending on how you looked at it, the bucket we were in jostled again as Cade brought it to the ground, nudging my attention off of Lucy. Amelia rushed over, just as Lucy started to climb out.

"Are you okay? Oh my God, I can't believe..."

"I'm fine. Can't you see..."

Their words crossed over each other. Meanwhile, I wrapped my hand around Lucy's good arm. "Easy. Let's get you out without jostling that break."

Lucy spun in my direction, her eyes snapping. "I..."

Amelia cut her off. "Don't be silly. Let Levi help you," she ordered.

Amelia was the only woman I knew who might be bossier than Lucy. She was also close to six feet tall and tough as nails. Gorgeous too with her amber hair and eyes, and leggy, curvy build. She was like a sister to me. Good thing because Cade would probably kill any man who took a fancy to her.

He must've gotten out of the truck because he materialized at Amelia's side. I didn't wait to give Lucy any more time to debate how she was getting out. I climbed out swiftly and reached over, lifting her against me.

Her eyes collided with mine. For a flash, it was as if we were alone. With her body bundled up in my arms, she was warm and relaxed against me. The temptation to drag my tongue along the delicate skin along the side of her neck was so great, I had to grit my teeth.

Reality intruded in the form of Amelia demanding to know if Lucy's arm was okay. I reluctantly eased Lucy down and stepped back.

"We need to get your arm looked at," I said, my voice coming out gruff.

Lucy's eyes flicked to mine again, the air going heavy in an instant. My body hummed in response to the electricity snapping between us.

"That's it," Amelia announced. "Let's go."

She all but dragged Lucy with her, calling over her shoulder at the last minute.

"Tell your dad I'm driving as fast as I want to the hospital."

Cade chuckled, his eyes catching mine. "Only Amelia would think she could get advance permission to speed like a madwoman."

"Well, your dad *is* the police chief."

We returned to the rescue truck and headed back to the station. I was unsettled and bothered I hadn't been the one to take

Lucy to the hospital. Which was completely ridiculous. I might've had a thing for her for too damn long, but this urge to protect her, that was something different.

On the drive back, we got a call to a fire on the outskirts of town. There went the rest of my day.

Chapter Two

LEVI

Hours later, going on one in the morning, I stripped down at the station and took a hot shower. I was the last one of our crew at the station. After showering, I made sure everything was locked up in the back and was about to leave when I heard a voice from the reception area.

I walked to the front and found Lucy sitting in the waiting room. She'd obviously showered since I'd seen her a few hours ago. Her blonde hair was damp, and she was wearing a t-shirt and a pair of swingy cotton pants. A removable brace was on her forearm.

It was rare to see Lucy in anything other than her construction gear. Lucy might almost look like a fairy, but she was one of the toughest women I knew. I'd had a thing for her ever since I moved to Willow Brook right after high school. She'd ignored me then, and she mostly ignored me now. Those moments today when I helped get her off the roof were probably the longest amount of time I'd spent with her alone.

I pushed through the door into the waiting area. "Hey Lucy, what's up?"

She glanced toward me. "Maisie let me in a little while ago and said I could wait," she said, referring to our call dispatcher. "I just wanted to thank you. Seriously."

Maisie didn't usually work late, but her fiancée, Beck, had been on duty with us at the fire tonight.

I was surprised to see Lucy. She tended to treat men like they were gum on her shoe, myself included. She stood up as I walked toward her. My body tightened—the way it always did when she was around. She was quiet, two red spots appearing on her fair cheeks. She was usually ignoring me, arguing with me, or glaring at me. It was so rare to not have her doing that, I had to soak it in for a minute.

She couldn't be much over five feet tall, if that. She was slender, but curvy. No matter how hard she tried to hide her curves under baggy clothes and her battered construction outfits, it was impossible not to notice. At least for me.

Ever since the first time I met Lucy, I'd been drawn to the bundle of contradictions she was. She was an electrician and a kick ass builder. She could probably hold her own on any construction crew given her skill, yet she'd joined Amelia's small business and bought into it. They were one of the most sought after construction companies in town due to Amelia's high-end architectural designs, their solid work and the fact they refused to expand. They took only a few projects every summer and turned down far more than they accepted. Lucy looked at home in her usually worn jeans and t-shirts paired with leather work boots.

With her fair skin, blonde hair and sky blue eyes, her looks belied her personality. At a glance, if you didn't know, you would think she was sweet based on her angelic appearance. Her nose was pert and tipped up at the end. She had fine cheekbones, her brows arched delicately, and she had thick blonde lashes framing her wide blue eyes. To top it all off, she had plump, lush lips. Fuck. Not the best idea for me to stare at her. My cock twitched.

She looked apprehensive as she stared back at me. She swallowed, the sound audible in the quiet room.

"Well, that was all," she said.

"What was all?"

"That," she said, circling her hand in the air. "I just came to say thanks."

She shifted on her feet and adjusted her shoulders, her eyes flicking away from me and back again. A wave of protectiveness rolled through me. What the hell was it about her? She just got to me. It wasn't simply that I wanted her—because holy fuck did I want her. When I saw her like this, I wanted to protect her, although I couldn't tell you why. It was so rare for her not to be ignoring me or arguing with me, I didn't quite know what to do with the feelings welling up inside.

"You don't have to thank me, Lucy. It's my job," I finally said.

She nodded, fiddling with a ring on her hand. "I know, but still."

She went quiet, snagging her bottom lip with her teeth and worrying it. My cock did more than twitch now. I took a breath, willing my cock down. It ignored me. As long as Lucy kept chewing on her bottom lip, I was going to have to get a handle on myself.

I nodded again, trying to stay laser focused on the moment. "No problem." I gestured to her arm in its bright blue brace. "How's your arm?"

"Oh, it's good. No break, but the doctor thinks I bruised the bone. They didn't even put a cast on it. Just this thing. It'll be a pain in the ass for work, but I'll make do."

"Glad you're okay."

She started to turn away.

"Don't go out that way," I said quickly. "I don't have the key to bolt this door from inside. I've only got the one for the back. Follow me."

She swung to face me again, and it occurred to me this was one of the rare times I'd seen her with her hair down. It was almost always stuffed up under a baseball hat or pulled back in a ponytail. I'd had no idea how long it was. The damp golden locks tumbled in waves around her shoulders and halfway down her back. She was breathtaking.

She nodded, her cheeks still flushed, and followed me as I led the way into the back area. We reached the main door to the crew parking area, and I held it open for her. As she walked by me, she unintentionally brushed against me. A jolt of electricity hit me at the brief point of contact. I took a breath and shackled my need, quietly letting her pass before closing and locking the door behind her.

I glanced around the parking lot, expecting to see the little blue truck she drove. When I didn't, I looked to her. "Where's your truck?"

She shrugged. "In the shop."

"Need a ride?"

She took a deep breath and let it out before looking to me and away. She shrugged. When she looked back to me, her cheeks were flushed.

"No thanks." She paused before continuing. "I told off my landlord," she said bluntly, a little laugh following.

That came out of left field, but I burst out laughing. Leave it to Lucy to tell off her landlord.

"What the hell for?"

She was actually laughing, a rare sight for me. She had a husky, throaty laugh, which didn't help the state of my body. On the heels of her laugh dying down, she shrugged.

"He's a fucking asshole, and he wanted to almost double the rent for next year. It's not that I can't afford it because I probably could, but he just pissed me off. I told him to fuck off. Until I find another place, I was planning to do some serious couch surfing. I'll figure something out."

I wasn't sure how we got from her truck to this. "I think you might've missed the deadline for couch surfing tonight."

One of her small shoulders lifted in a slight shrug. "I'll call Amelia."

I couldn't quite believe the next thing I said.

"You can stay with me."

I swear, I wasn't offering to get her into my bed. Hell, I knew the odds of that were slim. The words slipped out. It's what I would offer any friend. As soon as I spoke, the implications became clear in my mind. Any proximity with Lucy was probably not a good idea for me.

I must've startled her because her mouth actually dropped open. She snapped it shut, her eyes narrowing.

"I don't need anywhere to stay," she said quickly. "I'll call Amelia and see if I could crash there tonight. She'll pick me up."

My mouth almost fell open. Because it was that ridiculous for her to call Amelia now, considering it was past one in the morning.

"You haven't called her yet?" I asked.

Lucy shook her head. Either she didn't even think about her conundrum until it was too late to ask, or she was being stubborn. No matter what, it was too late to call Amelia. Not to mention Amelia and Cade lived a good twenty minutes outside of town.

"Lucy, at least stay at my place for tonight, okay?"

She eyed me skeptically. After a beat, she nodded.

Chapter Three

LUCY

I fidgeted in the passenger seat of Levi Phillips' truck. I didn't know what the hell I was thinking when I agreed to crash at his place. The only reason I said yes was because it was late, or rather insanely early in the morning. I didn't want to bother Amelia at this hour and try to find a way to get out to her and Cade's place when it was a twenty-minute drive. I hadn't thought to call Amelia sooner, which annoyed me to no end.

All in all, I was having a shitty week. I'd swallowed my pride—big time—before stopping by the fire station to thank Levi for his help this afternoon. My entire evening was a big mess between spending time at the hospital to get my arm checked, and then going home only to get into an argument with my landlord and summarily being asked to leave because my lease ended today. The events tonight capped off a week already on the skids.

I stayed quiet and tried to calm the restless energy I felt. I hated needing help, but the truth was I had no great plan for a place to stay on short notice unless I really inconvenienced Amelia. I looked out the window as we drove along. The moon was bright, casting a silvery glow on the mountain ridge in the distance. Swan Lake, a massive lake that served as the centerpiece of Willow Brook, was visible to one side of the road. The town's namesake was a brook that meandered down from the mountains and fed into Swan Lake. The town's founders had followed the brook to the lake, hence the town's name.

The lake glimmered under the moon with the lights of various fishing and hunting lodges reflected in its still, dark waters. Levi turned onto the highway leading out of downtown Willow Brook. He seemed content with the quiet, which was a relief.

I was curious to see where Levi lived. I had a vague idea, but I'd never seen it.

Willow Brook, Alaska was a small town with a massive summer population. Tourists poured through town all summer long to hunt, fish, hike, bike, and more. With the town's proximity to Anchorage, roughly thirty minutes away, it was slightly inland with all the benefits of the mountains and an amazing view of Denali in the distance. We were within proximity to the ocean as well, so visitors could get their ocean fix too. Downtown was quite cutesy. It was an old mining town and had spruced up with lots of cute shopping and restaurants to keep the travelers happy. We got the benefits of a small town with the money of a bigger town.

Aside from the tourism, the town was small enough for the locals that everybody had an idea of who was who and who lived where. All I knew was Levi lived on the west side of town. As he drove through the moonlit night, I wondered to myself what the hell I'd been thinking. Just being this close to him made me jumpy, restless, and hot and prickly all over. Levi had been on a kick a few months back to try to get me to go out to dinner with him. He annoyed the hell out of me, but he'd finally dropped it. I suppose the reason he annoyed me was because he was sexy as sin. My body sure thought so. My mind might not be in agreement with my body, but I couldn't seem to curb the sweet heat that rolled through me whenever I was near him. I hated feeling out of control like that.

Danger, danger.

The heat coiling low in my belly was precisely why I tried to keep my distance from Levi. It was no easy feat, seeing as we shared many friends. Romance in general wasn't my thing, but trying to do anything like a relationship in the fishbowl of Willow Brook was annoying beyond reason. Everyone thought they had your best interests at heart, but God help me.

Everybody knew everybody here. Lately my friends were dropping like flies. Amelia had gotten back together with the love of her life, Cade, when he came back after seven years away. Thank God he came back though, otherwise she probably would've married an idiot she didn't even love. I might not have been an expert on romance personally, but I knew what I saw.

Anyway, I digress. Levi was hot, like make-me-stupid hot. He had dark honey blonde hair and deep blue eyes. I didn't want to think he was hot, but there was no sense in arguing with myself over it. Here I was, planning to crash on his couch apparently. This had the makings of a *very* bad plan. I hoped he was involved with someone else now. I made a conscious effort not to think about him, so I'd missed any gossip, if there was any to be had, on his relationship status.

The minute I thought that, disappointment stabbed at me. Even though he'd annoyed me with his attempts to get me to go out with him, a teeny, tiny part of me had enjoyed the attention. Ugh. This was how ridiculous he made me feel.

As we drove, he started to make small talk, chatting about the weather, the fire outside of town, asking me about a few construction projects and whatnot. Basically just being a polite and decent human being. I couldn't shake the restlessness and nervousness inside. Time alone with men was something I generally avoided. I wasn't a prude, but relationships just weren't my thing. Every so often, I had a one-off one night stand, but that was it.

Levi holding me in his arms when he kept me from falling had felt so good, and I could hardly think about how it felt. It was the modern world now, and I didn't need to care if I was turning into an old spinster, but part of me did. At twenty-eight, I was headed straight for plenty of years of being by myself. I hadn't meant to go this long without dating, or anything even remotely resembling it. Something happened, and I meant to get past it, Yet, I never did. I stuffed it into a box in my heart and in my head and decided it was best left there.

Despite my pulse running along at a wild patter and that inconvenient prickly sensation I felt inside whenever I was near Levi, I managed to make small talk as he drove. He turned down one road and then another before looping into a small circular driveway. It was late summer in Alaska. That meant the sun hardly ever set. At going on one-thirty in the morning, darkness had fallen, yet with the almost full moon high in the sky, it lit up the area around Levi's home with a silvery glimmer. There was a small pond in a field to one side. His home was rather cute. I felt his gaze on me and then he chuckled.

I swung to him.

"What so funny?" I asked, willing my pulse not to lunge when I met his eyes.

It was hard to keep that from happening. He had obscenely beautiful eyes—a deep, sapphire blue. He had no problem with straight on, direct eye contact either. Sometimes it felt as if he could see right through me.

"You look surprised. I live in a decent place, is that what's surprising?" he asked with a low laugh.

I couldn't help but return his grin. I didn't know what I'd expected, but it wasn't this. He had a small home with a wraparound porch set at an angle on the property. The front of the house had a wall of windows stretching up to the second floor. It was stained a soft shade of gray with purple trim. The moonlight made the purple seem brighter somehow.

"It's the purple that surprised me," I added, gesturing towards his house.

He flashed another grin, making my belly do a little flip. "Yeah, that was my sister's choice."

I vaguely knew he had a sister. She didn't live in Willow Brook, otherwise I probably would've known more. He climbed out of the truck and before I realized it, he was opening my door. My spine stiffened, and I glared at him, annoyed he'd done that.

"It's not like I can't get the door, you know."

He chuckled. "Yeah, I had to beat you to

it. I'll be honest. I was trying just because I knew it would get under your skin."

I wanted to be angry, but it was funny. That's how shameless Levi was. He didn't even try to hide his intent. I looked up at him and my breath caught. He was too handsome for his own good. He might as well have been in one of those sexy firefighter calendars. He had a rugged, almost regal look to him paired with a rock, hard body. He had a blade of a nose, sculpted cheekbones and a strong jaw. There was a scar that ran along one of his cheeks, making me wonder how he got it. It gave him an edgy quality.

I gathered myself, tamping down my annoyance because I didn't want him to know how much he got to me. With him holding the door as I climbed out of the truck, I could actually feel the heat of his body. His presence was strong and solid. He was the kind of man who made me want to lean into him. Strength made me nervous though, so the moment I felt that, I got skittish inside. I wanted to dart away like a startled deer. I managed to contain the urge as I stepped past him.

The sound of the truck door closing behind me was loud in the quiet. I heard wings beating through the air and glanced up to see a raven, dark in the silvery moonlight, flying just above us. I took a breath, the scents of Alaska summer washing over me—the cool air with the subtle hint of the ocean not too far away and the earthy richness of all the greenery.

I walked at Levi's side up the steps to his house. I noticed he didn't even bother to lock his doors when he opened it, holding it for me. I filed that thought away. I noticed little things like that because I always locked my doors. He flicked on the lights once we were inside. I paused to look around. I was again surprised, but figured perhaps his sister might've also cast her touch in here.

"Nice place," I commented, taking in the space.

We'd entered into the kitchen. An L-shaped counter separated the kitchen from the living room. It had barely hinted lavender granite counters, stainless steel appliances, and light maple cabinets. Seeing as I spent most of my days building houses, I noticed details like this. I knew he'd spent a pretty penny on those cabinets, and they looked custom. The floor was tiled in a silvery gray tile with a hint of lavender to it. The tile met hardwood flooring in the living room. The living room had a cathedral ceiling and a soapstone woodstove in the corner of the room. A sectional couch was to one side and a TV on the opposite wall. Stars were winking in the sky outside the windows, the moonlight illuminating the field and small pond.

I spun around, looking upward. A railing circled all three sides, except for the one with the windows. There was a single door on each of the three walls. I presumed those were the bedrooms. There was only one door downstairs, which must've led to a bathroom. Levi stepped past me.

"Come on, I'll show you the guest room," he said.

"Oh, I can sleep on the couch."

He stopped and glanced at me, his eyes narrowing.

"You're not sleeping on the couch. I actually have two bedrooms. You'll have one all to yourself if that's what you're worried about."

Oddly, I wasn't worried about that. I opened my mouth to argue. I had no problem admitting I could be contrary, especially when it came to Levi, or any guy for that matter, trying to suggest what I should do. I snapped my mouth shut when I realized the futility and the silliness of it all.

I shrugged, feeling a little sheepish. "Okay."

His rich blue gaze held mine. I felt like he could see right into me, and I looked away because I didn't like how exposed I felt.

"I'll show you upstairs," he finally said before turning away.

I followed him up the stairs.

"Bathroom," he commented, pointing to the door in the center back wall. "My bedroom's over there," he added, gesturing to the left before leading me to the door on the opposite side.

We stepped into a spacious bedroom. It was furnished simply with a bed and two night stands. The furniture was light maple with clean modern lines. The bed had a cream-colored, fluffy down quilt with pillows piled high. The room was sparsely decorated with a few landscape photos.

I felt his gaze on me and looked over at him. When he didn't say anything, I felt compelled to speak. "This is nice. Thank you. I'll be out of your hair first thing tomorrow. I'll call Amelia for a ride and..."

His gorgeous blue eyes narrowed again. "You're not calling Amelia for a ride. That's ridiculous."

He looked truly affronted I'd even suggested someone else give me a ride. For a flash, I felt a little bad, but my annoyance at his assumption he could tell me what to do was stronger.

"If I want to call Amelia for a ride, I'll call her for a ride."

I huffed, I actually huffed, and then spun around.

Levi put his hand on my shoulder, pausing me from stomping away, which was what I wanted to do. His touch was like a brand. That single point of contact was hot and sent sparks of heat through me. I was so rattled at my body's reaction, I didn't yank away.

"I'll give you a ride wherever you need to go in the morning, okay?"

His tone was a tad less authoritative this time. I was too annoyed with myself at my reaction to him to carry on. I was also exhausted, my arm ached, and I desperately wanted to sleep. I needed to burrow into the covers and forget everything. Most particularly, forget how much my body was drawn to Levi. I nodded. "Okay."

His eyes held mine again. God, I wished he wasn't so comfortable with direct eye contact. Just now, his gaze felt soft, as if though he could sense how unsettled I was. He let his hand drop and stepped out of the room.

"Good night," was the last thing I heard as he closed the door.

I stripped out of my clothes and crawled into bed. The sheets were cool, and the quilt light and soft over me. I drifted into sleep, thoughts of Levi tumbling through my mind.

Chapter Four

LUCY

I woke up, feeling more rested than I had in years. For a moment, I was disoriented and then I remembered I was in the guest bedroom at Levi's house. Given the events of yesterday, it was a miracle I'd slept as deeply as I had. I rolled onto my side and looked out the window, which faced the field in front of the house. Mist was rising off the tall grasses as the sun rose above the trees, its rays landing on the dewy landscape.

I took a deep breath and let it out. I had no idea what time it was. I didn't have my purse, or frankly anything. I'd left my purse in Amelia's truck when she took me to the hospital to have my arm looked at. I lifted it, relieved to experience only lingering soreness when I carefully shifted my wrist inside the brace. I sighed, recalling I'd subsequently gotten into a fight with my landlord and had no good plan for where to stay. Finding a new apartment in the summer in Willow Brook was no easy matter. Most places were booked to capacity with tourists.

It was so odd Levi had been the one who helped me yesterday. I hated thinking of what happened in these terms, but rescue me he did. I briefly wondered why he'd ceased his teasing attempts to get me to go out with him and then forced my mind off of those thoughts. Romance wasn't in the cards for me. It didn't matter that Levi made my body feel all kinds of crazy. Restless, I kicked the covers off and hopped out of bed. I dragged my t-shirt on and put my ear to the door. It was still early, so I was hoping I could sneak to the bathroom.

When I didn't hear anything, I slowly opened the door. Levi's bedroom door, directly across from me on the opposite wall, was closed. The house was completely quiet. I stepped out quickly and ran on my tiptoes to the bathroom, dashing inside and closing the door quickly.

I took care of business and tiptoed back out, only to find a brown and white hamster in the middle of the balcony walkway. It paused to look at me and then scurried over to sniff my foot.

What the hell? Levi has a hamster? Wow.

The incongruity of it made me burst out laughing. I leaned down to stroke my fingers over its fur. The little hamster wiggled under my touch and looked up.

"Ah, I see you've met Ham."

Levi's voice was low and gravelly, roughened from sleep. The sound of it sent a prickle down my spine. I stood quickly and spun to find him rounding the corner of the balcony.

Sweet hell.

The moment I saw him, heat unfurled in a wave through my body. Did I mention he was calendar material? I knew he was handsome, but my imagination had *not* done him justice. He wore nothing more than a pair of navy blue cut off sweatpants that hung low on his hips. His chest might as well have been carved from stone. Every muscle was delineated. He was so fit, it should've been illegal. My eyes soaked him in. I couldn't look away. My mouth went dry, and my pulse took off like a rocket.

All the while, I stood there with a hamster who decided to climb on my foot. I was so discombobulated, I'd forgotten I was wearing nothing other than a t-shirt. It hung just past my hips. When this fact occurred to me, I flushed straight through. I realized Levi probably had a perfect view of my bottom when I bent over to pet the hamster who was apparently named Ham. I was all kinds of hot and bothered. This ranked up there with one of the most mortifying moments I'd experienced. Ever.

I couldn't seem to snap out of it, just staring at him while heat bloomed in my center and radiated outward. If Levi noticed anything amiss, I couldn't tell. He closed the distance between us until he was right in front of me. Only inches away.

I wanted to touch him. Desperately.

My hand apparently had a mind of its own. Because I touched him without even thinking, reaching out and sliding my palm down his chest. His skin was warm, lightly dusted with hair. His rich blue gaze locked to mine. The air around us felt alive, shimmering and pulsing with need.

I couldn't seem to take my hand away, but I suddenly got anxious, nudged by my past and all the reasons why I didn't do things like this. As if he could predict my next move, he curled his hand over mine. His touch was warm and strong. His thumb brushed across my wrist in that spot where the skin was so sensitive, it made me ache. Hot shivers raced through me.

I swallowed, beating back against the anxiety building. Somehow it was mingling with the intense desire I felt and amping it higher and higher.

"Have coffee with me," he said.

I didn't know what I'd expected, but it wasn't this. He made no other move, simply standing there with my hand held in his and his thumb hypnotically coasting over the wild beat of my pulse.

"Okay," I blurted out.

He uncurled his hand. I had to force myself to take mine away. I instantly missed the feel of his warm skin under my touch.

His mouth curled at one corner. "So this is Ham," he said, gesturing to the hamster.

Ham had his haunches propped on my foot as he stared ahead. "Um, you have a hamster?"

Levi nodded. "I do. My sister gave him to me. She said I needed company."

"You let him run loose?"

I was hyper focused on this because I couldn't seem to get my body under control. With my channel clenching with need and my belly fluttering, it was all I could do to stay sane. I was also way, way too aware of how close Levi was and how insanely sexy he was. With his honey amber hair mussed from sleep and his glorious chest there for me to see, it was fair to say I wasn't thinking too clearly. At all.

He shrugged. God, even his shoulders were sexy, the muscles rolling with his easy shrug. "Yeah. He got out once and nothing came of it, so now I leave his cage open. He goes in and out and does his thing. Anyway, did you need the bathroom?" he asked, thumbing toward the door.

I shook my head wildly. "Nope. All set."

At that, I dashed off, desperate to create some distance between Levi and me and maybe, just maybe, get my body under control.

Chapter Five

LEVI

I shouldered through the doorway into Firehouse Café. Warmth and the scent of fresh baked goods washed over me. Firehouse Café was on Main Street in downtown Willow Brook, almost dead center in the middle of town. The café was housed in the town's original firehouse and had been renovated into a cheery space. The seating area was in the old garage with the garage doors turned into windows overlooking Main Street with Swan Lake—a massive lake and the main tourist draw in town—in the distance. The café was decorated with local artwork. Round tables were scattered in the seating area with the deli and bakery counter to one side.

As usual, the café was busy. From spring

through autumn, it was teeming with tourists. Come winter, it stayed busy with locals. The café had out of this world coffee and baked goods for breakfast, phenomenal sandwiches for lunch, and a damn good dinner selection. In short, Janet James, Firehouse Café's erstwhile owner, did a bang up job of making the place irresistible in all seasons.

Willow Brook was roughly forty-five minutes outside of Anchorage, just close enough to have the overflow of tourists from Anchorage and just far enough to feel like you were almost in the middle of nowhere. With Swan Lake sprawling in the center of town, Willow Brook was a hub for fishing, hunting, hiking, biking and then some. Wildlands Lodge, along with a number of smaller lodges, sat on its picturesque waters, charging a fortune tourists were happy to pay.

It was late summer with autumn already nipping at its heels. I scanned the crowded café and went to stand at the back of the line. The weather was clear today, hence the café was bustling with tourists grabbing coffee on the run before they headed out for whatever activity they had planned in the wilds of Alaska, while locals were scattered amongst the tables.

Despite my efforts to persuade Lucy to have coffee with me this morning, she'd shrugged me off when we got into town. Sensing that if I pushed too hard and too fast, she would push back even harder, I'd let it go.

Someone nudged my shoulder, and I glanced back to see Cade behind me.

"Hey man what's up?" I asked.

Cade flashed a grin. "Coffee, you?"

"Same."

"I'm guessing we'll be called in to help with cleanup from that fire yesterday," he commented.

"Yep. What time is your crew headed out?" I asked.

"I'll sort it out once we get to the station. I've gotta swing by Denali Builders first. Damn boiler broke last night."

We stepped forward together as the line moved.

"That sucks. Can you fix it?"

He shook his head. "Nah. We tried every-thing. Amelia bought it used when she built the house, so we knew it only had so many years in it. It's a $20,000 repair," he said with a slow shake of his head."

"Damn," was about all I had to offer.

"Even worse, Amelia spent the morning

on the phone trying to round up favors and see if anyone has one hanging around. No one local has a good one in stock. I mean, those are usually ordered as it is. I told her it'd be best if we bit the bullet and spent the money now for a good one. It'll be weeks before we get the replacement though."

"At least it's summer," I commented.

"True, but we have no hot water. Even worse, our hot water tank flooded when the boiler broke, so we've got a mess downstairs. Amelia wants to tear up the hardwood flooring and redo it."

"Well, if you need any help, just say the word."

Cade nodded. "Thanks, man. I can do the install myself. We've just gotta get the boiler here."

We stepped forward again when a large cluster in front of us finished ordering and moved away from the counter. Janet James looked up, bestowing a wide grin between us. It was pretty much impossible not to smile when Janet did. With her twinkling brown eyes, her round figure and her effervescent warmth, it suited her to be the center of the café.

"Well boys, what can I get for you?"

"Coffee," we said in unison.

Janet chuckled. "Anything special?"

"Whatever you've got as strong as you've got it," I said in return.

Her gaze flicked to Cade.

"Same," he said quickly.

"Nothing to eat?"

"Better get us a bag of your mixed pastries," I added. "We'll bring them to the guys at the station. We're looking at a day of cleanup."

After I paid and ignored Cade's attempt to pay for his coffee, Janet spun away to take care of our order, while we stepped over to the pick up counter. The bell above the door jingled cheerily, and I glanced over reflexively to see Lucy walking in. The moment my eyes landed on her, my body tightened in anticipation.

It had been a damn miracle I'd gotten myself under control this morning after I walked out of my bedroom to see her. I'd had an absolutely perfect view of her bottom. Not that I couldn't have guessed she had a sweet body, but she hid it well. She had a perfect heart shaped bottom in shockingly feminine pink cotton underwear. I'd about fallen over. Just seeing her now with that vision in mind sent a shot of lust straight to my veins.

I'd done some quick mental talk to keep

my cock down because I'd known the minute she spun around, my response to her would've been obvious, seeing as I'd been wearing nothing but a loose pair of sweatpants. When she did straighten and turn around with her gorgeous blonde hair a tousled mess and her t-shirt hanging just to her hips, I'd had to do some more mental quick talk. Even though her t-shirt had nearly swallowed her whole, her breasts pressed against it with her nipples easily visible through the thin cotton.

Then, she'd gone and touched me. From the look in her eyes, she had startled herself as much as she'd startled me. Usually I would've wanted to tease, but I'd stopped myself at the look in her wide blue eyes and the heat banked in their depths. A few months back when I'd been trying to cajole her into going out with me, I would have said there was a spark between us. Because it was damn near impossible to miss. Oh, I wouldn't lie and pretend I didn't want her for the challenge. But it was more than that. Whenever I was near her, the air felt electrified around us.

Yet, nothing could have prepared me for that brief moment with her. The air became heavy inside of a second. The intensity of her gaze and the intimacy in the moment had thrown me. I hadn't expected it. I sure as hell hadn't expected her to touch me.

I watched as Amelia followed Lucy through the doorway. Though Amelia towered over Lucy, Lucy's presence was so strong, I rarely noticed that detail. Cade called Amelia's name. The second she looked over, he winked, winning a smile from her. She couldn't have known how perfect it was that she and Lucy were here for coffee after Lucy had wiggled out of it with me.

"Grab us a table?" she called out.

Cade nodded and looked to me. "Mind getting those coffees?"

"Not at all."

It appeared he'd shifted gears and decided we were staying for a bit. But then, Cade was so whipped by Amelia, it wasn't the slightest surprise. Didn't matter they were married and had been for a good two years now, didn't matter he'd likely just kissed her goodbye this morning less than an hour ago. He'd want to steal more time with her. Worked for me because that meant I could steal a few more minutes with Lucy.

I snagged our coffees and strode over to the table he found in the corner. Within minutes, Amelia was threading her way over to us with Lucy. I watched as they approached, seeing a familiar guarded expression on Lucy's face. I wasn't prone to being a *feelings* kind of guy. Nah. I took an easy come, easy go approach to romance. I wouldn't say I was a player, more of a 'pass from one friendly dating relationship to the next' kind of guy. Yet, Lucy got to me.

She was so damn beautiful she took my breath away. She was the kind of beautiful that was impossible to miss. She tried so hard to hide it with her tomboy attitude and her bitchy armor. Up until Cade moved back to Willow Brook, even though I'd noticed her—because it was simply that impossible not to—I'd written her off as too standoffish and distant.

After Cade and Amelia got back together, my social circles had bumped into Lucy's in ways where I saw there was far more to her than the prickly cactus vibe she threw off. She was incredibly loyal to her friends and always quick to be there whenever and however her friends might need her. Yet, if there were anything other than a platonic vibe, she threw up walls like nobody's business. I'd been foolish enough to think I could charm my way through those walls. No such luck. Oddly, trying to charm her had made me *feel* things I wasn't too accustomed to feeling. I wanted to know why she was so protective, why she pushed so hard against me.

Until yesterday and then last night, I'd pretty much figured I needed to leave well enough alone.

Amelia reached us first. "Any luck?" she asked after dropping a lingering kiss on Cade's cheek and sitting down beside him.

"Nah. Earliest we're going to be able to get that boiler is in two weeks and that's if we're lucky."

"What's going on?" Lucy asked as she slipped into the chair beside me. It was the only chair left, but I didn't mind one bit having her a little close to me.

"Our boiler died last night, and our hot water tank flooded. I called everywhere this morning. Denali Builders has a shitty one in stock, but if we're going to spend the money, I want a decent one." Amelia paused to take a big gulp of her coffee. "So no hot water, and the floor is ruined where the water was," she said with a sigh.

"It's not like we can afford the twenty grand right now, but we're gonna take the hit," Cade added.

Lucy looked between them, her blue eyes worried. "Well, that sucks." She moved to lift her coffee cup with her injured arm and then rolled her eyes as she quickly switched hands.

Amelia's eyes narrowed. "How's your wrist?"

"Oh, it's fine. Just a little sore," Lucy said firmly. "Sorry about that mess. If you need help with the floor, let me know."

Amelia shrugged. "Not until you're cleared to use that hand again. We'll deal with it. We'll probably stay at Cade's parents until we get it fixed. I *hate* cold showers," she said emphatically. "Speaking of that, it rules out you crashing with us until you find a place. Once we get the boiler, you're welcome as long as you'd like though."

Lucy nodded and took a quick swig of her coffee, her purposefully nonchalant air belying the tension coming off of her.

Amelia's next suggestion made me want to kiss her.

"Why don't you crash at Levi's?"

She couldn't have known how perfect that was.

"Fine with me," I added, making a distinct effort to keep my tone casual.

"What happened with your landlord anyway?" Amelia asked next when Lucy nearly choked on her coffee.

"Well, you know my lease was up. He wanted to up the rent. Like a lot. I got into an argument with him about it, and then he said he wouldn't renew the lease. Since I'd blown off dealing with it, I had to leave last night."

Amelia grinned. "That's what you get for arguing about it."

Lucy rolled her eyes.

"Levi's got plenty of room," Cade said.

I beat back the urge to tease because I knew if I did, my chances of having Lucy take me up on the offer were substantially less.

Lucy finally nodded, her gaze catching mine. The hint of vulnerability flashing in the depths of her eyes tugged at me. If only because she likely felt cornered by the situation, I purposefully held back and said not much of anything.

Lucy had changed out of her delectable, almost see-through t-shirt and had on a pair of denim overalls atop a fitted t-shirt. She was so fucking gorgeous, and she tried so hard not to be that I loved it.

Conversation moved on with Amelia asking a few questions about the fire the night before and me asking about their latest project.

"Are you working today?" I asked, gesturing to Lucy's blue brace.

She caught my eyes, her gaze narrowing.

"Of course."

"I already asked her about that," Amelia said with a roll of her eyes. "She says she has one perfectly good arm." She pinned her gaze on Lucy. "Just don't do anything stupid."

Lucy took a giant gulp of her coffee and glared at her. "It's no big deal. It barely hurts today. It's a bone bruise, nothing more. I just have to wear this brace for a few weeks and that's it. I can work, and I'm going to work, so don't argue with me about it."

"Fine. Just don't get hurt again," Amelia retorted.

"We won't mind rescuing you if you do," I couldn't resist adding.

Lucy's glare swung to me. "I can't believe you guys. Are you telling me you wouldn't be working if you had one of these?"

Cade and I caught each other's eyes and then I shrugged ruefully. "Fair enough. I would do light duty."

"Is that what I call it then?" she asked with the barest hint of a grin.

Damn. Getting Lucy to sort of smile nearly did me in. I played it off with a laugh.

"Something like that. Probably no heights

and definitely not putting up those beams you were handling yesterday."

Amelia shook her head vigorously. "Absolutely not. You shouldn't have been doing that alone anyway. I've already called Max. He'll help for a little bit today, so we can finish those beams."

Lucy muttered something under her breath and took another gulp of her coffee. My cell phone buzzed, and I slipped it out of my pocket. Glancing down, I saw it was a text from Maisie, our dispatcher, ordering us to the station to respond to a non-emergency call.

"We need to get to the station," I said catching Cade's eyes.

Lucy and Amelia followed us outside. When Amelia stepped to Cade to kiss him goodbye, it was a the-rest-of-us-should-look-away kiss, so I glanced to Lucy.

"Are you going to need a ride to my place tonight?" I asked.

Her gaze looked downright mutinous.

"Actually, I need to pick up my truck. If you don't mind picking me up at our building site and dropping me off with my truck, that would be great," she said, her tone controlled. "I'll make some calls today and see if I can find a place, so I might not even need to crash at yours again."

I simply smiled and nodded, knowing damn well her chances of that would be slim this time of year. It was at the height of summer and everything was filled to the brim. I watched as she walked away with Amelia, wondering if I would manage to break through her defenses sometime in the near future.

Chapter Six

LUCY

I spent the day feeling cranky. I didn't like the fact I couldn't work at full force. I didn't like the fact I didn't have a place to stay. I fucking hated that I got cornered into saying yes to crashing at Levi's again. While Amelia and Max were busy dealing with the beams, I spent at least an hour calling everywhere I could think of to scout up a rental. Even Janet didn't have an extra room at the B&B she owned beside Firehouse Café.

Absolutely no luck on finding a way to wiggle out of staying at Levi's. If I was sensible, I'd be relieved he offered. But I wasn't. He made me feel funny and made me think about things I hadn't thought about in years.

Worst of all, he made me wish I wasn't lugging so much emotional baggage inside.

After reluctantly accepting it wasn't likely I was going to find a new place to rent on short notice, I got back to work. My attitude still sucked. I was annoyed with my sore wrist and annoyed with my life. After Amelia and Max got all the beams in place and climbed down from the scaffolding, Amelia strode over to lean against a sawhorse nearby as she guzzled some water. I'd been working on cutting hardwood flooring with the miter saw, something I could manage with my injured wrist. She took her work gloves off, slapping them on her jeans to knock the dust loose.

"Little early for that, don't you think?" she asked.

I glanced her way as I carefully made another cut. "I figure I might as well get done what I can. This way, we'll be ahead of the game once I'm back at it," I offered with a shrug. "We have dry storage on site, so it should be fine."

Max Richards strolled over, dragging his sleeve across his face and wiping the sweat off his brow. It was mid summer in Alaska, the only time of the year that anything resembling hot weather happened. He glanced my way, flashing a grin.

"I'm guessing you'll be relieved when your wrist is better. What happened anyway?" he asked.

Amelia didn't even bother to keep from rolling her eyes. "You know Lucy. She shouldn't have been up there trying to put the beams up herself, but she decided to try it. I went to town to pick up some extra lumber and got back to find her already up there. Lesson learned," she said bluntly.

I threw a glare at her, but I couldn't help but smile. I had known better, but I'd been impatient. "Yeah, lesson learned. The doctor said I didn't break it, but bruised the bone. I should be good as new in a few weeks," I offered.

Max chuckled. "Well, glad you didn't do more than that. I need to get going, so I'll catch you two later. Call me if you need an extra hand again."

Amelia threw a smile his way as he turned away with a wave. Max usually handled all of our excavation work on projects. He was a good guy and easy to work with. As annoyed as I was that we needed his help for this, I was glad for our sake he was around. Without his help today, our project would've been substantially delayed.

Amelia strode to our work truck after she drained her water bottle and returned with two more bottles of water. She tossed one my way, and I caught it with my good hand. Turning, I set my last piece of cut wood down and leaned my hips against the miter saw stand.

We stood in the quiet for a few minutes. I scanned the building site. It was a lovely lot on the outskirts of Willow Brook, nestled into the forest with spruce, cottonwood and birch surrounding the lot. The trees opened up beside a marshy field, offering a view of the mountains in the distance. A raven called with a magpie chattering in reply.

"How's your wrist feeling anyway?" Amelia asked.

"Fine actually. I was in a little pain this morning, but ibuprofen did the trick. It's going to annoy the shit out of me though," I offered with a little laugh.

She threw a wry smile my way. "Oh I'm sure it will. I might tease you about it, but I would be the same way. Any luck finding a rental?"

I took a swallow of my water and glanced

up at the sky. It was bright and sunny today, wispy clouds scudding across the blue sky.

"Nope, but I should've known. It might be close to fall, but it's still busy. Anybody that has a place available is busy making money hand over fist."

"So true. I can ask Cade's parents if you can stay there too. I realized after the fact you might not appreciate us saying you should crash at Levi's. He's a good guy, but I know he..."

Instantly, I got defensive. Amelia was my best friend, but I wasn't about to look like a chicken in front of her. Levi was a good friend of hers and Cade's and, well, of anyone and everyone I happened to be friends with in town. It would be weird if I got all uptight and refused to accept a friendly offer.

"No problem," I said quickly. "Levi offered, and there's no reason I can't stay there."

Oblivious to the fact I'd stayed there last night and he'd seen me in my underwear this morning, she continued, "He's actually got more room than we do anyway. I'm sure he'll let you stay as long as you need," she offered.

"Yeah, if he doesn't drive me crazy," I added, unable to resist that comment.

She rolled her eyes. "Levi's a good guy. He's just a flirt."

I knew that to be the case. What I didn't know was what the hell to do about the fact he made me hot inside and out and half-crazed in my brain.

———

Three days passed while I was staying at Levi's. Three days while his mere existence was driving me insane. I woke on day three, my skin flushed and a sheen of sweat covering me. I'd had another heated dream about Levi. It was the third night in a row when my body and my subconscious were betraying me in the worst possible way. My mind spun back to the memory of my dream.

Levi's lips on my skin, the scrape of his stubble on my neck and then down over my breast as his lips closed around a nipple. His muscled body pressed against mine. His cock, hard and throbbing between my thighs, sliding through my wet folds. I cried out...

Oh. My. God. I woke up crying out Levi's name. I shifted my legs restlessly under the sheet. I could feel the damp heat between my thighs, my core slick with need for him. In my sleep addled mind, I wasn't thinking clearly, or at all. Before I knew it, my fingers were dipping into the wet heat at my core. I was so horny. I hadn't been this way in... Hell, I'd never been this way. I was drenched, and I needed relief. I stroked through my folds, my skin flushed from my need and from my embarrassment at wanting Levi this much. He had invaded my dreams and was taking over all of my thoughts.

I buried my fingers in my channel, my sex clenching around them. This wasn't enough. I wanted what my dream gave me—Levi's cock buried inside of me. In my dreams, I knew what it felt like to be filled by him. My breath came in little bursts as I teased myself. I drew my soaking wet fingers out, sliding them back and forth over my clit, a swollen button of need. My orgasm was right there on the edge. On a burst of pleasure, I buried my fingers inside my channel again. My sex clamped down around them as my release washed over me, sharp, abrupt and intense.

I lay still, my breath coming in little pants. This was insane. I'd had an orgasm with nothing but Levi in my mind, and my fingers were sticky from my juices. I wanted to roll out of bed, walk straight into his bedroom and make my dream a reality. Last night's dream involved me riding him, his fingers digging into my hips as his cock filled me. My channel pulsed around my fingers again. I slowly withdrew them, rolling onto my side and trying to get a grip on myself.

I was in a conundrum. I'd had no luck finding a place to stay yet. I was in the awkward position of desperately wanting Levi and needing to get the hell away from him. Without somewhere to be, I didn't have a good excuse to leave. I was in the awkward position of Levi being a shared friend in the small social world of Willow Brook. Aside from staying with him, I didn't have any options except to break down and call my mother. Which absolutely wasn't an option. The moment that thought crossed my mind, I wanted to burst into tears.

I threw the covers off and strode quickly out of the room towards the bathroom. Ever since the first morning when I'd furtively tried to go to the bathroom without Levi noticing, I'd been very good about remembering to get dressed before I left the guest bedroom. This morning, I wasn't thinking. Hell, who could blame me? I'd just climaxed all over my own hand fantasizing about Levi. I could feel the moisture between my thighs as I walked to the bathroom. Before I reached it, yet too far away to dash back to my bedroom, Levi's bedroom door opened.

I froze. He scrubbed his hand through his messy hair and glanced up, his gorgeous blue eyes widening when he saw me. His chest was bare—his dangerously sexy chest that made my mouth water—and he wore cut off sweatpants that hung low on his hips. They weren't loose enough to hide his arousal. If only he knew how wet I was. His eyes locked to mine. We stood there for a beat, staring at each other. If he was embarrassed about his obvious arousal, it didn't show.

"Morning Lucy," he said with a nod.

His mouth hitched up at the corner as his eyes flicked down. It was as if his gaze was an actual touch. My nipples tightened when I felt the heat of it. I suddenly realized my favorite t-shirt to sleep in was thin and white. There was no doubt my nipples were visible through it. My pussy clenched at the look in his eyes.

"Morning," I choked out, trying to sound casual but instead sounding hurried and rushed.

Mortified, I dashed into the bathroom, nearly slamming the door shut behind me. Only then did it occur to me he probably needed to use the bathroom. I leaned against the door and tried to catch my breath.

"Do you need the bathroom?" I called out.

Oh my God. I sounded like I was in a panic. Inside I was. My heart was hammering so hard, I felt like it was going to beat its way out of my chest. I was afraid he could hear it from wherever the hell he stood.

"I do, but I'll go downstairs. No worries," Levi replied. Right outside the fucking door.

I sagged with relief at the sound of his footsteps retreating from the door. I took several shaky breaths, willing my pulse to slow and my traitorous body to get under control. After a moment, I pushed away from the door, belatedly turning to lock it. Silly and pointless, but a habit I couldn't break. I knew Levi was polite, no matter how much he teased me before and no matter how much it annoyed me. I knew he wouldn't barge in while I was in the shower. He just wasn't that kind of guy. But I locked the door anyway, almost as if to protect myself from my own desire for him.

I paused and looked at myself in the mirror. My cheeks were flushed, my hair was a wild mess and my naughty nipples were taut under the thin cotton of my shirt. I knew

Levi had gotten quite a fill of that little view.

Never again. I won't forget to change before I run to the bathroom again. So fucking stupid.

I rolled my eyes. Dammit. The only reason I was in such a tizzy this morning was because I had another crazy hot sex dream about Levi and masturbated thinking about him. On the heels of several deep breaths, my pulse finally started to slow. I heard the shower turn on in the bathroom directly below this one.

I couldn't help but envision Levi's cock outlined by his sweatpants, the soft fabric practically caressing his body—the cock that I desperately wanted inside of me, at least in my dreams.

There's a reason you can't think like this.

This voice whispered in the back of my mind. My desire was washed away in a wave of... I don't know what it was—sadness, regret and shame all balled up together maybe.

I rarely dated. I'd never had a boyfriend. Don't go thinking I was a prude. I wasn't a virgin, but the messiness of emotions wasn't something I could tolerate, so I limited myself to occasional one-night stands and nothing more. Tears pricked at the back of my eyes, and I spun away from the mirror.

Quickly turning on the shower, I gave the water a moment to heat up before climbing in. I let the hot water mingle with my tears as I showered. My mind spun back to a place I didn't like to think about.

Chapter Seven

LUCY

I was a freshman in high school in San Francisco, California. To this day, I don't know why we moved there, but we did. It was brutal for me. I'd always been the smallest person in my class. I'd been teased all through elementary school for my size. I was kind of shy, not shy like afraid shy, but more socially shy. My childhood had sucked. To put it bluntly, my dad was an asshole. He wasn't physically violent too often, but he was emotionally and psychologically abusive to my mother. He berated her constantly, to the point she was almost invisible. She had zero self-esteem and never spoke up for herself.

I was an inconvenient afterthought for my dad. When I was really little, he ignored me, and I thought that was hard. Until I got old enough for him to notice me. Somewhere in middle school, he started treating me just like my mother. I was too smart and that was stupid. Or so he said. Everything was stupid about me, according to him.

I never had any friends because there was no way I was going to bring them home. When I got to high school in the small middle of nowhere town where we lived in California, I managed to make one or two friends. Then, I was ripped out of that little town and plunked down in San Francisco at a hip, big city high school.

It was no surprise to discover I didn't fit into the new social order. I was still tiny and hadn't grown into myself at all. I had no curves, none to speak of. You could hardly tell I was a teenager. I didn't fill out until my junior year. There I was, shy with hardly any friends and with a mad crush on one guy. Floyd Lewis was dreamy and cool and everything I wasn't. He was a star football player. I told myself he was worthy of a crush because he was smart too.

I blushed every time I even looked at him. I was *that* socially awkward, and I knew he wouldn't pay attention to me. My nickname was Shorty, and I was the butt of plenty of jokes. I supposed I was passably pretty, but it seemed near impossible to be objective about myself in hindsight when it came to adolescence. All I knew was it was a socially lonely time and emotionally stressful.

Then, my crush asked me to the school dance.

There I was, little Lucy Caldwell, and the cutest boy in the school asked me to the dance. I was nervous, but beside myself and stupidly excited. Those few days of bubbly joy and I-can't-quite-believe-this-is-happening looked so ridiculous after the fact. Floyd was tall and strong and had girls swooning over him in the halls all the time. As word spread like wildfire through the halls of our high school that he'd finally graced one lucky girl an invitation to the dance, I got plenty of dirty looks from other girls. I didn't really have any friends, so it didn't sting as much as it might've. I ignored them.

I was floating on that silly, heady joy that only a girl who desperately wanted to fit in could feel when she thought maybe, just maybe, she might be.

The evening of the dance arrived, and even though I had worried Floyd wouldn't actually show up, he did. He even came to the door with flowers. He was quite charming with his slicked back brown hair and flashing dark eyes. He gave the flowers to my mother, earning him a glare from my father. In hindsight, I don't think my father knew how to interact with him. My father almost refused to let me go to the dance.

For once, my mother stood up for me. She begged him to let me have that one small thing. So I went. I couldn't say it was wonderful. I was too nervous for it to be anything really.

For the dance itself, Floyd tugged me around on his arm. I was more like a piece of his clothing than a person. He socialized, he laughed, he let other girls fawn over him, but he was gracious and polite. After the dance, he took me to a park where I'd never been and kissed me. My memories were messy and blurry. I was too overwhelmed with nervous anxiety to really feel much. I had no experience to judge his kissing. I was definitely an entirely inexperienced kisser, and I didn't want to lead on that was my first kiss, my first anything. Kissing moved to heavy petting to him tugging my dress up. None of this was bad. Oh, it was awkward, and he was a little rougher than I would've liked, but it was just that he lacked finesse. It simply was what it was. I'd sadly assumed a part of my mother's way of dealing with men, which was to acquiesce.

I lost my virginity in the back of a fucking car on the night of my first and only school dance. It wasn't horrible, but it wasn't fun, or intimate, or anything like that. It hurt, and I felt like an idiot, mostly because I didn't know what to do. Floyd was, well, he just was who he was. He seemed rather happy with himself after the fact. He kissed me on the cheek at the door, and I went to bed, barely sleeping.

The next day came, and I walked into school to find *SLUT* scrawled on my locker. Somehow between the night before and that morning, Floyd bragged that he took my virginity. The rumor, like so many others, spread far and wide through the halls of the high school. To this day, I didn't know if Floyd knew his bragging would result in my social shame, but it didn't really matter. I never spoke to him again.

Maybe I was a challenge to him. I learned after the fact that there'd been bets about whether I would go to the prom with anyone and whether I was a virgin or not. My social shyness bit me hard. Even worse, somehow my father found out. All the way up until sixteen, he never laid a hand on me physically. I walked home that day, and he blacked both of my eyes right in front of my mother, declaring that I had turned into the whore she'd been. He shouted he only hoped I didn't get pregnant because that was how she'd trapped him.

While those two black eyes had been awful, they sent my life careening down a different path. Despite my not-so-stellar home life, I was an excellent student and I *never* missed school. When I had my very first absence from high school, my guidance counselor sent the school resource officer to check on me. My father never bothered to think he needed to stay home, so he'd gone to work. So had my mother. The school resource officer called child welfare after I answered the door, and he saw my black eyes.

My mother was given a choice—me, or my father. They weren't going to let me remain in his care, so she had to decide. She chose him. I got shipped off to foster care for a year before she found the strength to choose me later.

Chapter Eight

LUCY

The following day, I leaned against a sawhorse at our current project with a sigh. A raven called from the trees nearby. I watched as it took flight from a cluster of cotton-wood, a dark shadow against the bright blue sky. I loved all of the seasons in Alaska, but I was particularly fond of late summer. A soft breeze blew across the lot where we were building. The property was nestled amongst rolling hills on the outskirts of Willow Brook. Denali was peeking above the trees in the distance. I stared into the field off to the side where fireweed was blooming. The common weed bloomed in waves of bright fuchsia flowers across Alaska in late summer, splashes of color in the already stunning landscape.

I turned to reach for my water bottle, reflexively with my right hand. When my brace bumped the bottle, I glanced down and glared at it.

"Angry at your arm?" Amelia asked as she approached from our work truck.

Her amber hair was falling down from a ponytail as she dragged her sleeve across her face. I rolled my eyes as I switched hands and snagged my water bottle. Amelia leaned against the sawhorse beside me, throwing a grin my way.

"I'm angry at my brace. It's annoying," I said.

"When do you get it looked at again?"

"Next week. There's no pain. I don't see why I can't just take it off."

She threw a glare in my direction. "Don't be stupid."

"It's just a bone bruise," I countered.

"Yeah, but you want it to heal right, so take care of it."

Amelia took a long swallow from her water bottle before looking my way again.

"Any luck finding a place?" she asked, shifting the topic.

She couldn't have known she selected the

only other topic that was more annoying than my mildly injured arm. I'd had another dream about Levi last night. I could hardly be around him without getting hot and bothered. I felt betwixt and between. He wasn't crowding me and gave me my privacy. It wasn't him. It was me. That's what made me so nuts in my head.

I didn't know what to do with how much I wanted him. I'd woken up so hot last night, I'd been forced to take matters into my own hands. Yet again. I was starting to feel as if he owned my body. He certainly owned my dreams.

I feigned a casual tone. "No luck," I replied with a shake of my head.

"It's a tough time of year."

"Is there ever a good time of year around here to find a place to rent?"

Amelia threw a wry grin my way. "Not really. Not unless you're buying. It's either short term winter rentals when they open up, or waiting until something better comes along. Have you thought about buying?"

"It's on my list. Maybe in another year or so, I'll have enough saved up for a down payment."

"Well, I'm glad you can crash at Levi's since our place isn't an option right now.

Seems like you two have been getting along okay."

I narrowed my gaze. "Why do you say that?" My tone sounded more annoyed than I intended.

She flashed a grin. "Because you haven't been bitching about him."

"Well, he hasn't been flirting," I said grumpily.

I didn't say aloud that fact was actually bothering me a little bit. I couldn't fucking believe I missed Levi flirting with me. He was being scrupulously gracious, and it was driving me insane. His lack of flirting was making me want him to the point I was actually considering just tackling him. Perhaps if I could get this crazy need for him out of my system, it would go away.

My sanity was definitely in question. This was absolutely the craziest idea I'd ever considered, but I was nearly on fire all the time around him. No matter how hard I tried, I couldn't seem to banish him from my thoughts. In fact, the harder I tried not to think about him and not to want him, the more I thought about him and the more I wanted him.

Amelia's chuckle distracted me, and I realized I'd completely lost track of our conversation. Conveniently, it was easy to recall what she'd last said because it was about Levi.

"You were so cranky with him, I think he gave up on flirting," she offered.

I masked my inner turmoil with a long gulp of water before replying. "Took him long enough."

Her phone rang, and she tugged it out of her jeans, effectively ending our conversation. She stepped away to take the call, while I spun around and started stacking the hardwood flooring I'd been cutting all afternoon. I'd returned to that project today, and we were close to having enough for the house. I stacked it on a wheeled cart and left it in our covered storage. We finished up for the day with Amelia heading off to have dinner with Cade and his parents.

As I drove back towards town, I contemplated whether to stop and grab something to eat. Willow Brook had done wonders for me when it came to my social life. I'd been able to start over here for my last year of high school. Maybe I didn't have a ton of friends, but no one here knew anything about the slut shaming I'd suffered through at my last high school even though I was far from a slut. I'd made a few friends in Willow Brook, and when I started working with Amelia after college, she became my best friend. Her small circle easily enveloped me. I still wasn't much for doing things out and about on my own. I would occasionally grab coffee at the Firehouse Café. We had girls' night card game every few weeks, and sometimes I went to Wildlands, a local favorite bar and lodge, when friends were going.

It was Friday evening, and none of those things were happening. Usually this wouldn't matter at all. Except that meant going out to Levi's and worrying about whether or not I was going to see him. Part of me was nearly desperate to see him. Another part of me was annoyed and angry about my desperation and my body's betrayal. My stubborn side didn't want to dare let his presence dictate what I did.

Tonight, my stubborn side and my desperately wanting to see him side won this battle. I drove out to his house bound and determined to act like I didn't give a damn. When I pulled up and saw his truck wasn't there, I breathed a sigh of relief. And promptly wondered what the hell he was doing. That's how ridiculous I was over him.

I knew he wasn't seeing anyone right now because I'd made a sarcastic comment about women drooling over him the other night.

He'd taken affront and made a point to say he wasn't seeing anyone right now.

Grumbling to myself, I let myself in the house as Levi had assured me it was fine to do. He'd also made a point to let me know he'd do the same for any friend if they needed a place to stay. I still hated needing help and occasionally considered calling my mother. That was a quick *no* every time it crossed my mind.

Working in construction, even light duty work with my brace, left me plenty dusty, so I headed directly upstairs for a shower. I was relieved my brace was easy to remove for showers. Even though I was bitching about having to wear it, I wasn't stupid, so I immediately put it back on after I dried off. As soon as I stepped out of the shower, I knew Levi was home because I could hear the shower running downstairs. Simply knowing he was near caused my body to tighten in anticipation. Dressed in loose sweatpants, fluffy socks and a sweatshirt, I considered hiding in my room. Yet, that was silly, and I felt like a coward for even considering it.

I stomped down the stairs into the kitchen. Over his objections, I'd stocked up on groceries the other day. He insisted it wasn't necessary, but I didn't really care. I had to do something in exchange for having a place to stay. As I stared into the cabinets, I heard the water turn off in the downstairs bathroom. I settled on heating up a can of soup. I wasn't the best cook by any stretch. While I was hunting for the right size pot, the bathroom door opened.

At the sound of his footsteps, I reflexively looked over my shoulder. It felt strangely intimate to know he'd been naked in the shower with nothing but a thin door between us. My body had all kinds of feelings about that.

The moment my gaze landed on him, it was like a flash fire in my body. His mere presence was a match to the banked coals inside of me. He was bare chested with nothing but a pair of jeans on. Of course, they hugged his body like a lover, caressing every inch of his muscled thighs. I swallowed, my face flaming hot. My eyes, my willful, naughty eyes, lingered on the hard, sculpted planes of his chest. His chest was lightly dusted with caramel colored hair, barely visible over his amber skin. My hands itched to touch him.

I managed to drag my eyes up to his face, only to see his gaze darken when mine collided with his. I took a ragged breath and willed my pulse under control. It wasn't listening. At all. Butterflies spun in my belly and heat spread through my veins. My channel was slick and wet instantly. This was how ridiculous I was around him.

I managed another breath and swallowed. "Hi," I choked out.

Fuck. My voice was all breathy. Inside, it felt as if I was swimming against a tidal wave of need. My willful desire had embedded itself into my thoughts day and night. It was incessant and making me think crazy thoughts. For example, I was seriously considering just tackling him.

My need for him was a force I'd never faced. I'd never even been tempted like this. Outside of my father who I hated, I'd never had this much consistent proximity to any man. Beyond my first not-so-great sexual experience, I hadn't had many other experiences. I'd tried dating a few times in college, but found it was easier to keep things brief and physical. Marginally satisfying one-night stands let me keep the emotional boundaries clear. At twenty-eight now, I had to think—hard—about the last time I'd kissed anyone. It was beyond embarrassing.

Aside from the darkening of his eyes, Levi gave nothing away. He stepped into the kitchen, walking with that easy swagger of his. It wasn't conscious, no matter how much I wanted to tell myself it was. He was all man, a man on octane fuel with a body made of pure muscle. Not because he worked out for vanity. As a hotshot firefighter, he was the toughest of the tough. His work demanded the innate strength and confidence he carried. Hell, he had it in spades. My eyes greedily absorbed the sight of him as he moved closer.

He leaned his hip on the counter, apparently not even intending to put a shirt on.

"What's for dinner?" he asked, curling one hand over the edge of the counter.

"Soup," I said, holding up a can of tomato soup.

His eyes flicked to the can and back to me, widening slightly. "Soup?" he repeated.

My head bobbed in a wobbly nod because my body was humming, and I could hardly think. "Uh huh."

I prayed he couldn't tell my cheeks were flaming hot. I was fairly certain he could because my complexion didn't hide blushes very well. I didn't think this qualified as a blush. More like I was on fire inside and out and about to melt at his feet.

"How about I cook dinner?" he asked.

"Huh?" was my brilliant response.

"How about I cook dinner? Doesn't really seem like you cook."

Hints of a grin appeared at the corners of his mouth.

I stared at him, uncertain how to respond. This was the first night where I had nothing to do and nothing to eat when he was also here.

"You cook?"

His mouth stretched into a slow grin. My low belly clenched, need coiling tightly in a knot at the apex of my thighs. Sweet hell. His grins were dangerous. I was practically drooling. Meanwhile, he stood there, entirely oblivious to my internal state.

"Yeah, I cook. I love to cook actually. I'm pretty damn good at it."

I laughed because I was so startled I didn't know what else to do.

"Is there something wrong with a man who cooks?" he countered, still grinning.

I shook my head quickly. "No, not at all."

"Do you mind if I cook then?"

"Of course not. Cook whatever you want for yourself."

His eyes narrowed, and his grin faded. "I'll cook something for both of us," he clarified.

"Oh no. You don't need to do that. I'll just have soup."

I was starting to feel frantic inside. Overwhelmed with burning desire for him, muddled, out of my element and just all a mess inside, I didn't know how to comprehend any of this.

Levi reached out and took the can of soup from my hand, his fingers brushing against mine and sending a hot jolt of electricity through my body. My breath caught and my pulse took off like a rocket. Mind you, it wasn't like it was calm to begin with, but now it had gone completely crazy. I felt insane. Before I could form another word—because speaking wasn't really my forte, especially not right now—he returned the soup to the cabinet.

While I was busy trying not to melt on the spot, he got busy pulling things out of the refrigerator. He said a few things, none of which I heard.

"Lucy?"

Even his voice was sexy, like honeyed whiskey. It sent a shiver over my skin.

"Huh?"

My vocabulary had degenerated to this.

He grinned, sending my belly into another flip and heat spinning through my veins. "I'll have this ready inside of a half hour. Okay?"

"Okay."

Wow. I'd graduated to two syllables. Still grinning, he spun around and got to work. Uncertain what to do with myself, I slipped into a chair at the kitchen table. I was hot all over and my panties were wet. Apparently, he was going to cook shirtless.

If I got through this night without mauling him, it would be a miracle.

Chapter Nine

LEVI

I didn't know how the hell I did it, but I cooked dinner without dragging Lucy into my lap and kissing her senseless. Thank fuck, I had something to do. I meant what I said to her earlier. I loved to cook, I always had. All of my childhood memories involved cooking, mostly because that was where my family spent time together. I'd absorbed my parents' love of food. I was pleased to say, even a bit cocky about it, that out of my parents, my sister and my extended family, I was the declared best chef in the family.

While I cooked, Lucy sat at the kitchen table watching me. She was wound so tight, she was practically vibrating. The desire between us was heavy in the room. I sensed she was pissed about the existence of that desire. To keep my body in check, I busied myself cooking. I whipped up a simple dinner of chicken quesadillas. She'd done the funniest batch of shopping I'd ever seen. Her choice of groceries informed me she likely didn't cook. She got this hodgepodge of things, none of which really went together.

Thank goodness she'd gotten some chicken breasts, tons of cheese and tortillas. When I served her a plate and sat down across from her, her eyes flicked to me, widening. Her sky blue eyes caught mine and reeled me in. I found myself lost in her gaze on a fairly regular basis over the last few days.

"Oh wow. You can really cook."

She looked down at her plate and then back to me.

"You haven't even tasted it yet," I said, unable to resist a grin and a wink.

Her cheeks flushed. Damn. I loved it when she blushed.

"Well, I will now," she said quickly.

Inside of a second, she was moaning, which did not help matters with my body.

"Oh my God," she mumbled between bites. "You really can cook."

I chuckled. I'd seasoned the chicken with chipotle peppers and a blend of spices. I'd sprinkled fresh cilantro and topped them with a dollop of sour cream and cheese, and it was delicious. For a late summer evening, it was the perfect meal.

Lucy devoured everything on her plate. For her small size, she could put away some food. She insisted on cleaning up, all but swatting my hands away when I tried to help. I decided it wasn't worth arguing the point. After putting everything away in the dishwasher, she spun around, her hands on her hips. Her hair had dried in curly waves while I cooked. Not a lick of make-up on, and she was gorgeous. I loved seeing her with her hair down.

Of course, even her comfortable clothes swallowed her up. Yet, her generous breasts were impossible to hide. I figured she'd die on the spot if I let on I could see her tight little nipples pressing against the soft cotton of her sweatshirt. It was a damn good thing I was sitting down, otherwise she'd see exactly how hard I was for her.

She stared at me for a moment, her gaze considering. "Levi..." she began, her words trailing off.

"Yes Lucy?" I countered when she didn't say anything else.

She stepped closer to me where I sat at

the table. I was trying to be a gentleman. Hell, I'd called on *all* of my gentlemanly impulses over the last few days. Trying to give her space, trying not to tease. I knew in passing from Cade she hadn't had a lick of luck finding a place to stay yet. Which was quite all right with me. Except for the fact that she was driving me slightly crazy. Not because I minded having her around. Rather, the problem was I wanted her. Badly.

The more she was around, the more of a mystery she became to me. She was wound so tight and so guarded. Initially, I'd been drawn to her because of the challenge she represented. Oh and the plain fact that her mere existence near me was like throwing a lit match into the need burning inside of me.

I still wanted her, but now I wanted to understand her. The more time I spent around her, the more I sensed her underlying vulnerability. I watched as she stepped closer yet again, her tongue swiping across her bottom lip.

Oh fuck. She needed to *not* do things like that. She was only about a foot away from me with her eyes locked to mine. The flush on her cheeks deepened, and she worried the hem of her sweatshirt between her thumb and forefinger. Without thinking, I reached over and curled my hand over hers, wanting to ease her restless energy. Her breath drew in sharply when I touched her. Hot damn. That point of contact was like a bolt of lightning.

"What are you so anxious about?" I asked, the question slipping out unbidden.

"I'm not anxious," she said quickly.

I wasn't so sure about that, but I wasn't inclined to press the point.

Lucy's eyes held mine, the blue flashing dark, and the air around us fairly snapping. I expected her to tug away when I'd unconsciously reached for her. After all, this was Lucy, the woman who had dismissed all of my flirting and teasing as if I was nothing more than a gnat to swat away. Hell, if I hadn't had more confidence, she'd have easily made me feel like an idiot. That was all before I got to know her better.

It wasn't as if she'd chatted much with me over the last few days. Simply being around her and realizing her prickly exterior was a defense, I could see the softness underneath. Underneath was also a fiery, passionate woman. That's what had drawn me to her before. My proximity to her had only heightened my sense of her. My body's response to her was raw and primal.

I'd forced myself to take a step back and not engage in my usual teasing manner. If only because I had to keep myself on a very tight leash. My grip on that leash slipped just now, my reflex to ease her restlessness overpowering everything else. Yet now that I'd actually touched her again, the contact was a jolt to my body, striking me at my core and electrifying the air around us.

Lucy stared at me, her lips parting and her breath hitching again. Fuck me. She was the sexiest woman I'd ever known. I tried to order my hand to release hers. Yet, my hand wasn't listening. The sky blue of her eyes darkened almost to navy. I could see her pulse fluttering along the fair skin of her neck. Her nipples were tight, and it was all I could do not to tug her to me and tear that sweatshirt off of her, so I could feel her curves against me.

Surprisingly, her hand relaxed in mine. Moving solely on instinct, I reeled her to me. I wasn't thinking. At all. She was so small, a petite bundle of curves. Inside of a hot second, she was standing between my knees, her face just above mine where I was sitting. I almost laughed. Because I loved that about her, the contradiction of her petite size, her delectable curves, her fiery personality, and the sheer power of her presence.

Since I wasn't thinking, I sure as hell didn't expect her to reach out and trace her fingertips along one of my brows and then down along my cheek to my jaw. The trail of her touch was a line of fire on my skin.

"I hate that I want you," Lucy said, her eyes flashing.

"I don't." I countered. "In fact, I love it."

I stared at Levi, watching as his mouth curled into a grin, my belly executing a slow flip at the sight of it. Inside, I was a storm of emotions and need. I hadn't been able to resist touching him. He was a beautiful man. In a rugged, elemental way. My fingertips had come to rest along the stubble at his jawline. His lips were beckoning me. If I'd thought I could get a grip on myself and the need roaring through me, I was so very, very wrong.

At the sight of his dangerous grin, my belly tightened and need spun tightly inside. I was hot all over, so hot I could barely stand. I felt like melted wax near him, the fire between us softening me, while also making me want him more than I'd ever wanted anyone in my life.

I tried to be angry, but his grin was irresistible. Before I knew it, I was grinning in return. His hand had been holding mine right beside my hip. He eased his grip, his palm sliding around my hip and cupping my bottom.

"There's nothing wrong with wanting someone Lucy," he said.

I knew that of course. There absolutely wasn't anything wrong with wanting someone. I just hated how out of control I felt when I was near him.

I wished my brain had a fire alarm. I needed one, one just for Levi. The alarm could go off and let me know I needed to run. But I couldn't hold the heat back. The need inside built with such intensity, I couldn't turn away. So when he pulled me a little closer as he sat there—still bare chested, mind you—all of my defenses were useless.

I stood there, my body humming and my sex clenching. I could barely breathe as my pulse pounded so hard and fast, I was certain he could hear it.

Somehow, the act of him cooking me dinner—such a domestic, mundane event—

had struck me at my core and wiped away the last of my resistance. My hand slid into his hair, and I dipped my head. If I was going to be stupid, I might as well go all in. The moment my lips met his, I went from hot to burning. I hesitated at the point of contact. In all honesty, I hadn't had a ton of experience with kissing. It was too intimate, so I avoided it as much as I could. It was fair to say no man had blown me away with kissing. But Levi. Oh. My. Fucking. God.

Levi's hand cupped my bottom more firmly, pulling me flush against him. With him seated in the chair and me standing between his knees, every inch of his muscled chest was against me. It was glorious. I could feel his cock hard and hot just below the apex of my thighs. I'd wanted to touch him for forever it seemed. My burning, raw, aching desire could no longer be held back. One hand slid down over his muscled shoulder while the other coasted across the sculpted planes of his chest. I ignored my bulky brace. If Levi even noticed it, he didn't give any indication.

It felt as if he were waiting a beat to see what I was going to do. When I moaned at the feel of him under my touch, a low growl escaped from his throat, and his grip tightened as he pulled me closer. His tongue swept into my mouth, eliciting another moan from me. Sweet hell. I felt like I'd been waiting forever for this kiss. His lips were soft and mobile, his command of our kiss complete. By no means was I passive. My body was moving on its own as my tongue tangled with his. I couldn't get close enough fast enough. Suddenly, he tore his lips free and leaned back.

"Lucy," he said, his gravelly voice sending shivers through me.

I managed to open my eyes, so stunned I'd kissed Levi, I almost couldn't speak. My heartbeat was thundering in my ears. I could feel the moisture between my thighs. I was so aroused, I could barely think past it.

His gaze was locked to mine, the rich blue darkened to navy. Simply looking at him made my sex clench. We stared at each other, our breathing ragged in the quiet kitchen, the hum of the dishwasher the only other sound in the room.

"Do you want this?" Levi asked.

I swallowed, my mind a jumble, my internal state a tornado of need, sensation, and confusion. I wanted to say I didn't want this, but I wanted it so fiercely I couldn't bring myself to say otherwise.

I struggled to catch my breath, all the

while I couldn't force myself to move away from him. Being close to him felt too delicious. Hot and hard, so much better than my dreams. And let me tell you, those had been some *amazing* dreams.

When I didn't say anything, he leaned back, his hand loosening in my hair.

"I'm only asking because you did tell me to fuck off before," he said bluntly, his gaze holding mine.

His words felt like a dare. I swallowed and gathered myself. "I know," I finally managed to say, my voice coming out in a breathy whisper.

"So you don't want to tell me to fuck off now?"

I stared at him, trying to jumpstart my brain. But thought was hard to come by. I felt my head shaking back and forth before I realized that's what I was doing. Still, he simply looked at me.

"In your court," he said softly.

My heart was pounding so hard, it felt as if it was going to fly out of my chest. The need for Levi was coiled so tightly inside of me, it was a force beyond reckoning. I told myself to step back, but I couldn't. I didn't want to move away from him.

Rather than words, I slid my hand back

up to his hair, tangling my fingers in his silky locks and dipping my head. It was strange, as small as I was, to have him seated and me standing almost level with him. It felt as if he was trying to make sure I consciously did this. That was both empowering and annoying as hell. Because I wanted to forget myself, to lose myself in this and in him. Then his lips were on mine again and his hands were pulling me close. His fingers traced along the curve of my bottom, so close to that sweet spot between my thighs, I almost cried out.

He slipped a hand under my sweatshirt, the calloused surface of his palm sending sparks skittering along my skin as a low moan escaped. I barely recognized myself. I was frantic, anything to meld myself with him—with Levi, a man I'd desperately tried to persuade myself I didn't want.

In the far reaches of my mind, a voice whispered, reminding me I'd wanted him from the start and that's why I'd hated when he flirted with me. Something about my first sexual experience had messed with my head. It wasn't as if it was awful, but something about that event colliding with my father hitting me had fucked me up inside. I wasn't afraid of sex. I'd even had it more than a few times since then, yet every encounter was rather ho-hum. The electricity I felt with Levi, that subtle hum in my body with him—as if I was a tuning fork for him and him alone—was something I'd never felt before.

Aside from the whacked part of me when it came to sex, I was determined not to depend on any man. Ever.

I'd seen firsthand how that went for my mother. It was a disaster. But the fire flashing into flames between Levi and me was stronger than my determination to stay away. I couldn't think rationally. My defenses were burning to ash. All I could think of was the feel of Levi's hard body under my touch, of the hot need knotted at the apex of my thighs, and a few too many dreams where he'd been buried deep inside me.

I dimly came into awareness, straddling his lap. His cock was hard and hot against my pussy through the thin fabric of my sweatpants and the denim of his jeans, so insistent, so present, and so hard and thick.

Levi murmured my name as his mouth closed over one of my nipples, sending pleasure in a jolt through me. I felt crazy. Something about him saying my name nudged me out of the wild place inside. For a flicker, awareness sliced through. I realized what I'd been about to do. I dragged my eyes open to see my sweatshirt on the floor. My nipples were damp from his wicked tongue. I ached for him, every inch of him.

Startled, I scrambled off of his lap and snatched my sweatshirt off the floor, tugging it over my head, swearing when the sleeve caught on my brace. I knew I looked like a wild woman. My hair was a mess, my clothes were barely together, and I was flushed all over.

I looked toward Levi. He hadn't moved from where he sat on the chair. His golden hair was a tousled mess, his eyes dark, and his lips damp. My willful eyes trailed over his chest, landing on his lap where his arousal was blatant. I hadn't even realized I'd torn his jeans open. His cock was outlined against his black briefs. He was the sexiest man I'd ever seen.

I needed to get the hell out of here.

"This wasn't a good idea," I said abruptly.

Oh. My. God. I sounded like a crazy idiot. Levi simply nodded. For a beat, I thought he was about to say something. I didn't wait. I spun away and dashed up the stairs.

I actually ran away from him. Slamming the bedroom door shut behind me, I tried to catch my breath.

Oh my God, I can't believe I just did that.
What the hell was I thinking?

I scrubbed my hands over my face and pushed away from the door quickly, locking it and crossing my arms across my chest. I began pacing in a semi circle around the bed. Fuck, fuck, fuck.

I was mortified, so embarrassed I could hardly calm down. It suddenly occurred to me that Levi could probably hear my frantic pacing. I plunked down on the end of the bed, curled my knees up against my chest and hugged them, staring at myself in the mirror across from the bed. I didn't know how I calmed myself down, but I managed. Mostly because I had no other choice. The worse option was to try to face Levi. I convinced myself a night of sleep might help me forget that I'd come within a hairsbreadth of fucking him. He'd been right there with me, every step of the way.

Chapter Eleven

LUCY

I fell into a restless sleep, my body still reverberating from the echoes of desire. I came awake later, rolling my head sideways to look at the clock. It was just past one in the morning and blessedly dark. Even in late summer, the days were still long in Alaska. The sun didn't set until close to ten at night.

I woke from another heated dream about the one and only star of my dreams the last few nights—Levi. My panties were drenched, simply moving my legs sent a streak of pleasure through me as I lay there trying to catch my breath. I wondered if it was actually possible to have an orgasm while you were asleep. It was that bad. My body felt as if it were on the precipice of one. This was the fourth time that I'd woken from a crazy hot sex dream and wanted to bury my fingers in my pussy.

My good hand had a mind of its own, and in seconds, my fingers were teasing between my thighs. I gasped at the slick wetness, my hips arching into my own touch. But it wasn't enough. And I knew it. I didn't want to be a coward. More than that, I wanted Levi with such ferocity, I couldn't deny it.

I kicked the sheets back and stood. My mind was fuzzy from sleep and nearly delirious with need. I wore nothing other than a thin cotton t-shirt and panties. I dashed out of my bedroom and around to the other side of the loft.

Levi slept with his door partially open. Slipping into his bedroom, a shadow scurried past my feet, and I realized it was Ham. He was a rather adventurous little hamster. Not even his presence nudged me out of my state. I was going to see this through and excise Levi from my thoughts.

I walked to the side of Levi's bed, looking down. He was on his back, one of his arms thrown over his head. The sheets were bunched at his waist. I wondered fleetingly if he had dreams anything like the dreams I had.

Crawling onto the bed beside him, I trailed my fingers over his chest. I didn't wait, my body was too restless. Straddling him, I almost groaned aloud to discover that his cock was already hard. My drenched panties and the thin sheet covering him were the only thing between us. My pussy throbbed knowing how close I was to finally finding release.

I felt when he came out of his half asleep state, his body tensing slightly before he shifted and brought his hands to grip my hips lightly.

"Lucy?" he murmured, his voice rough from sleep.

"It's me," I replied, feeling a grin curl my lips.

I had to admit I liked waking him up like this. A bit too much. I didn't want to talk though.

I rolled my hips and leaned forward until I was about an inch from his lips. My eyes had adjusted to the darkness by this point. There was a night light in his bedroom, casting a soft glimmer across the bed. He'd mentioned in passing that he kept night lights throughout the house because he'd almost stepped on Ham one night. Right now, I was glad for it because there was just enough light for me to see the desire reflected in his gaze.

"I changed my mind," I said.

"About what?"

"That this is a mistake. I still hate that I want you. But I want you."

His hands tightened on my hips, sliding around to cup my bottom. My own hips rolled reflexively as a low moan escaped. I couldn't help it. I was so close.

"I don't hate that you want me," he murmured. His gruff, sleepy voice was so sexy, it sent a hot shiver through me. "It's not a mistake either."

Then his hands were sliding up my back, my shirt bunching at his wrists as he tugged it up and over my head. He was careful with my arm, which kind of annoyed me. I didn't want to have to worry about it, and it didn't hurt. But I was too frantic and too beside myself to think much about anything other than getting him completely naked and having him buried inside of me. My need for that specifically was so strong, I knew it wouldn't be filled until he was rooted deep within me.

Everything was a blur. His hands and mouth were everywhere. Oh, and he slept naked. That was a pleasant surprise. My breasts were heavy and aching, my nipples so tight they hurt. He teased me to madness, rolling his thumbs across my nipples, his mouth drawing one and then the other inside, his teeth scoring them lightly. When I got impatient and tried to shove the sheet out of the way, he chuckled.

"Oh no, we're not rushing this."

He spun us over and stretched out beside me. I rolled my head to the side to catch his eyes.

"Not what I want."

His laugh was soft against my skin as his lips trailed down my neck and teased my nipples, taking his sweet time.

"Oh are we gonna do that again?" he murmured.

I didn't know what it was about him, but everything was foreplay. Even his words.

"Do what again?" I choked out as he mapped my body with his mouth.

"You're gonna tell me this was a mistake and run off."

I shook my head swiftly. "No. I have an end goal in mind."

His laugh sent sparks dancing along my skin, the scrape of his stubble on my belly making me crazy.

"Always in a rush, aren't you?"

I couldn't say why, but I was comfortable. I was caught in this moment with him and didn't really care to let my self-consciousness ruin it. So I laughed, and then he was dropping kisses between my thighs. He pushed my knees apart, and then his mouth was on the most intimate part of me.

I gripped his hair and hung on for dear life. He made love to my pussy with his mouth. Teasing through my folds with his tongue, swirling around the hot button of need, and burying his fingers inside my channel. His touch was so much better than mine. I lost sense of everything, but the feel of his fingers driving in and out of my channel and his tongue making me crazy.

He gripped my hip with one hand as I bucked against him, chasing after that sweet release. He drove his fingers deeply once more and sucked my clit into his mouth. Pleasure spun tight and then let loose, flying through my body. The force of my climax was so intense, I was nearly limp by the time he drew back. His fingers were still buried deep inside me when I felt his gaze.

"Lucy."

Chapter Twelve

LUCY

When Levi said my name, his voice strummed a chord in my body, which reverberated along the ragged edge of my heart. I was too tangled up and too lost in need to allow myself to dwell on it. For a beat, it frightened me. He touched a place inside that I never wanted to be vulnerable. But I couldn't look away.

The moment he said my name, I opened my eyes to find him rising above me. Every inch of him was hot, hard and breathtaking. Even though I'd just had the most explosive orgasm I'd ever had with a man, it wasn't enough. It wouldn't be enough until he was inside of me.

Even though I couldn't seem to form

words, my body knew what it wanted. My legs were curling around his hips to hold him close. I found my words when he rolled to the side.

"Where are you going?" I murmured, trying to stall his motion with one of my legs.

He chuckled, his low laugh sending my belly spinning into flip after flip after flip.

He reached for his nightstand, and inside of a second, he was rolling a condom on and shifting over me again. I was far beyond being embarrassed about how desperately I wanted him. There was no point in hiding it. Maybe, just maybe, once would be enough, and I could stop dreaming and fantasizing about him. His hands slid up my sides catching my hands in his and stretching them up over my head.

He caught me rolling my eyes when he was careful with my braced wrist.

"What's that for?" he asked, a grin teasing at the corners of his mouth.

"I won't break. Especially since this..." I paused and wiggled my hand in his "...is in a brace. It's fine."

He held my gaze, his eyes darkening. "Deal with it."

His elbows rested at my shoulders. Framing my face, he released one of my hands. Brushing my hair back, he held my gaze. The moment was so intense and so intimate, I felt naked in more ways than one. Yet, I promised myself I wouldn't be a coward, so I didn't look away.

"Now would be the time to tell me to stop," he said, his voice gruff.

I was so screwed.

All he had to do was talk, and I melted even more. I felt like liquid wax inside, hot and pliant. All I knew was I needed him inside of me. I needed to be that close. My pussy clenched, my core throbbing for more.

I curled my legs around his hips and nudged him, but he held firm. I had to face it, he was far stronger than me. No matter how much I wanted to make him do my bidding, I couldn't. His mouth hitched at the corner, sending my belly through another series of flips.

His gaze sobered. "I'm serious. If you aren't sure, just tell me."

My heart thudded inside my chest, hard and fast, and I swallowed against the wave of emotion rocking me. All of a sudden, this felt far more real than anything I'd ever experienced. I was far past trying to pretend I didn't want him. In the face of what had just happened, I would look like a big fat liar.

So I held his gaze. "I know. I don't want to stop."

For a moment, Levi was silent and still, and then he adjusted the angle of his hips and rocked into me. His cock, every hard, thick inch of it, slid through my slick folds. It didn't matter I'd just climaxed all over his face, I was already at the edge again. He wasn't one to be rushed. I was learning that about him quite thoroughly.

Only when I moaned his name and bucked against him again did he finally draw back, adjust the angle and then start to slide into my channel. He moved slowly, as if concerned he would be too rough. I'd admit, it had been long enough since I'd had actual sex that I was tight, tighter than I expected. It wasn't painful, but... Well, I was small, and he was big.

His speech was slurred when he spoke. "Lucy, you feel so fucking good." He caught my lips in a kiss as he held still inside of me for a few beats. I could feel the pounding of his heart against my chest. On the heels of a breath, he sank to the hilt, seating himself deeply.

He drew back, his eyes catching mine. It was almost too much. We were as close as two human beings could be. I couldn't say I knew what to expect because I didn't. I hadn't allowed myself to think about this. It was only something from my dreams. This was so real, so intense, and so much better than my dreams. I rocked against him as my body relaxed, adjusting to the delicious stretch of him filling me.

He moved slowly at first. He was surprising me in so many ways. I hadn't expected him to be anything other than a fun guy in bed. I hadn't been prepared for the way he would savor every inch of me, for the way he would be careful of my arm, of my body, and how he would treat me as if I was made of spun glass, while also being a touch rough and dirty.

Once I began to rock restlessly against him, arching and sliding my good hand down his back, my nails scoring him, he didn't hold back anymore. It became fast and furious because that was what I needed it to be. My want was so great, and my need ran so deep.

"Fuck, Lucy. Take it easy," he muttered. "I don't want to hurt you."

My eyes whipped open. "You're not. Levi, please just..."

Since I couldn't find the words, I rocked against him. He answered with his body, drawing back and surging deeply. I couldn't look away, though I meant to. Locked in his navy gaze, the pressure gathered inside, like a wave rolling into itself. He reached between us. With a swirl of his fingers over my clit, the wave crested and I spun apart inside, my climax crashing through me. I felt him tighten and distantly heard my voice calling his name, feeling his eyes on me as he called mine before collapsing against me.

We lay there, skin to skin, heartbeat to heartbeat, as we caught our breath. I didn't remember falling asleep. Yet, I woke in the night, warm and relaxed. Levi was curled up behind me, his palm splayed on my abdomen. I told myself I should get up, but I couldn't.

Chapter Thirteen

LEVI

The early dawn light filtered through my windows. I'd forgotten to close the curtains last night. Needless to say, I'd initially gone to bed sexually frustrated beyond belief. I'd eschewed taking matters into my own hands. With Lucy so near, I knew it would simply be unsatisfying. Then she'd gone and surprised the hell out of me.

My mind spun back to last night. I was curled up behind her, and I'd woken up with a hard-on. It only made sense. I might've found some release last night, yet what I'd thought would be a fun roll between the sheets had been far more.

Instead of satisfying my appetite, it had only served to whet it further. Lucy, petite though she was, was a bundle of curves. With her luscious bottom pressed into my cock and one of her breasts cupped in my palm, it was impossible for my body not to respond. She was sound asleep, her breathing steady. It wouldn't have surprised me to have woken and found her long gone. In fact, I was slightly surprised that wasn't the case.

I decided to do exactly what I wanted and not overthink any of this. So I thumbed her nipple, grinning when it puckered under my touch, and slid my hand down over her belly and the curve of her hip to dip between her thighs. She was soft and warm, her legs shifting in her sleep to give me access. I dusted kisses along the curve of her neck. Damn. She tasted so good—sweet with a hint of musk. Her personality could be so prickly, yet the sweetness underneath was such a surprise it made my heart clench.

I heard her breath hitch just as I slid my fingers through her curls and into her folds. I found her hot, wet, and ready. I almost chuckled because she made me want to tease though I knew she wouldn't appreciate it. She tensed slightly, and then I dragged my thumb across her clit. She sighed, a little breathy moan escaping.

The sounds Lucy made? Fucking heaven.

She was an expressive woman. I'd known she never hesitated to tell anyone what she thought about anything. To see her expressive side when she was wild with need nearly slayed me.

I couldn't hold back my grin when her breath hitched again as I sank a finger, knuckle deep, in her channel. I had no illusions she was a virgin, but she was tight enough last night, it wouldn't surprise me to learn it had been a while for her. I distantly wondered if she was sore and considered whether I should ask. She moaned again, her hips rolling into my fingers, and I forgot everything else. I knew what I wanted.

To taste her.

So with my fingers still buried between that sweet spot at the apex of her thighs, I shifted my weight and rolled her towards me with my free hand. Almost forgetting for a moment about the brace on her wrist, I paused when it bumped against me. Lifting my head away from where I'd been dragging my tongue over the curve of her shoulder, I glanced to her.

"You okay?" I asked.

Her eyes opened, snagging mine and making my breath catch and my heart give a resounding kick to my ribs. Fuck. Her eyes were so damn gorgeous. Just now, her sky blue gaze, hazy with sleep and desire, blinking under the sun filtering through the windows, set my heart to thudding hard and fast. I was so screwed. She had me by the balls, and she didn't even know it. Her eyes narrowed and she glared at me.

Perfect, fucking perfect. I loved it when she was a little annoyed. I'd freely admit her feisty side was a big part of my attraction to her. Oh, I wasn't so stupid as to deny that she was fucking gorgeous. Because she was. But I loved how she bristled and how sarcastic she was. I loved the contradiction of how, at a glance, you might think she was fragile and then she opened her mouth, and you discovered the opposite.

"I'm fine," she said.

I think she meant for her words to sound annoyed, and there was a hint of it in there. But with the look in her eyes, she sounded breathy. As I drew my fingers back and sank them into a channel again, her pussy clenched around them, and my cock hardened even further.

"Good to know," I said, not even bothering to hide my grin.

I moved swiftly, dusting kisses down Lucy's body and bringing my lips to the core of her. She tasted salty and sweet, the center of her like honey and musk. I couldn't get enough. Still fucking her with my fingers, I set to teasing her to madness with my tongue. I could've done this for hours, but she came quickly in a noisy burst, her channel clamping down around my fingers. I rose up and rolled off the bed swiftly, scooping her in my arms and leaning down to snag a condom out of the drawer I'd left open last night.

She bumped her heels against my thighs. "What are you doing?" she demanded.

But then she giggled, and my heart squeezed again.

Lucy just did it for me—in so many ways and on so many levels. I hadn't expected last night to happen. In fact, I'd resigned myself to the reality that nothing like that would ever happen with her. To have last night, to wake up and be able to kiss her all over and have her giggling as I carried her into the shower, well, it was damn near close to heaven.

"We need a shower," I said as I nudged the water on with my elbow.

As soon as steam started to fill the room, I started to step into the shower.

"Hey, I need to take my brace off."

I stepped back quickly with her still in my arms. Because honestly, I didn't want to let go. I quickly helped her take it off, setting it on the counter by the sink carefully.

Her eyes on mine, she asked, "Planning to put me down anytime?"

"In a sec."

As soon as we stepped into the shower, I let her slide down as I quickly rolled the condom on with my now free hand. She started to turn around, but I slid my hands over her luscious bottom. Without another word, she got the message. Her palms flattened against the tile wall, she arched her back with her lush ass tilting up for me. I didn't need to check to see if she was ready because I knew how wet she was. I slid my fingers between the sweet cheeks of her ass, spreading them and then positioning my cock at her entrance.

I held still for a beat, my cock fisted in my grip and dragged it back and forth in her folds. She moaned, and I started to slide inside. Her body tensed slightly, and I paused.

"Too fast? Are you okay?"

Lucy looked over her shoulder, her golden hair damp now and her eyes flashing. She shook her head swiftly. "Oh my God! I'm fine."

As if in emphasis, she wiggled her bottom and pushed back against me, bringing my cock all the way into her core.

I let out a low growl, losing myself in the feel of her. I meant to make this last, to drag it out, but I couldn't. Not with her rolling her hips back into every stroke, not with her channel throbbing and clenching around my cock. Before I knew it, my release was thundering through me with heat tightening at the base of my spine and my balls. I reached around, dipping my fingers through her curls and swirling them over her clit. She cried out, her channel milking my release as it roared through me. My knees almost gave out at the force of it.

Thank fuck there was a wall beside me. My palm slapped against it as I gripped her hip with my other hand. I heaved, trying to catch my breath and holding onto her as I slowly came to.

When the thundering of my pulse eased and my breath slowed, it occurred to me that I didn't want to move. I'd die a happy man if I could stay buried inside of Lucy forever.

No such luck. She glanced over her shoulder, a grin curling the corner of her mouth.

"Well that was fast," she said.

I couldn't help but chuckle. "It's your fault."

Still buried inside of her, I watched as her eyes widened slightly.

"How so?" she asked.

I eased my grip on her hip and slid my thumb over her clit again, teasing in the folds of her pussy just above where my cock was filling her.

She groaned, her channel clenching again.

"It's too good. You feel too good," I said for emphasis.

Her cheeks flushed, and she looked away. Having regained my balance, I slid my palm down her spine, slick from the water raining down upon us. Realizing I couldn't stay buried inside of her forever, no matter how much I wanted to, I drew back slowly. I quickly disposed of the condom, leaning out of the shower to toss it in the trashcan by the sink.

When I turned back, she was already soaping up. Just looking at her with soap bubbles rolling down her skin and her lush body flushed and pink from the steam, my cock twitched. It was a damn miracle, but I could probably go another round already. Yet, I sensed we'd already barreled too far and too fast, far beyond where Lucy had ever wanted to go with me.

So I behaved like something other than the raving lunatic I was for her. We showered, we dried off, we dressed, and then I made breakfast. I was stunned that she didn't leave earlier. I finally had to leave first when a call came in from the station. I offered to give her a ride, but she shook her head.

Just as I was about to jog down the steps to my truck, I reflexively turned back to where she stood waiting on the deck. The urge to kiss her was powerful, a current I almost couldn't withstand. Yet, I sensed her withdrawal and held back.

———

I went to work that day, Lucy filling my thoughts whenever I had a spare moment. Later in the afternoon, we had a call for a fire that had flashed out of control again in a nearby stretch of undeveloped forest. We'd been dealing with this fire on and off all summer. This happened often in Alaska. There were so many large swaths of undeveloped forest, the fires could restart after we got them under control. Wind and other events could whip them back into a frenzy.

My crew, along with Cade's, responded. It was a long afternoon of establishing new firebreaks. A group of hikers had decided it wasn't worth following the no campfires rules set for this area and then the wind shifted again.

When we returned to the station late that evening, I was starving, filthy and exhausted, along with my entire crew. After a quick shower, I was walking out into the back area when I saw Amelia pulling Cade close for a hug. It was nothing unusual. In fact, an afternoon like this was par for the course in being a hotshot firefighter. I was well accustomed to the sight of my fellow firefighters being greeted at the end of a long day, or when we flew back in after weeks out in the wilderness fighting fires.

Something about last night and something about Lucy made me wish she were here to see me today. I gave my head a shake. I'd be lucky if she hadn't packed up and left my house this afternoon without telling me. I strolled over, greeting Amelia after Cade pulled away. There were several guys lounging around the break room table.

Cade leaned his hips against it and chatted casually with them.

Amelia caught my eyes. "Thank God you've got a place for Lucy to stay right now."

"Oh?" I countered.

"Well, yeah. We just found out the boiler we want has been back ordered, so it's going to be another three weeks. We already paid for it. If we try to order a different one, the wait might be even longer, so we're still camping at Cade's parents. Lucy still can't find anywhere to rent. It's the worst time of year. Honestly, early summer is better. Because at least then she might be able to sweet talk somebody out of their summer rental. But right now, everybody's all booked up," Amelia explained.

I nodded, biting back the urge to grin. Amelia couldn't know how damn happy I was about that. Because I was hoping for so much more with Lucy than what I had last night and this morning. Yet, I didn't know what Lucy had told Amelia about us, if anything. I had enough sense to keep my mouth shut on that topic.

With a shrug I replied, "She's welcome as long as she needs. I keep telling her I'd do the same for any friend."

Beck Steele came strolling out of the locker room.

"Hey action hero," I said.

Beck had picked up that nickname after an elderly woman he rescued declared his name sounded like an action hero's name.

Beck rolled his eyes. "I'm no action hero. If I am, we all are."

"Wildlands, guys?" Cade asked, his eyes scanning the cluster of us.

What I wanted to do was call and see if Lucy wanted to meet us, but I knew I might be pushing it with that. I also knew it might raise a few eyebrows if I said no because I almost always grabbed a beer and dinner with the crews. So I nodded. Other voices chimed in, and we all tromped out to head over to Wildlands, a local favorite hangout and tourist hotspot.

I caught Amelia's eye as she climbed into the truck beside me. "You headed that way too?"

She nodded. "Yup. Lucy and Maisie are already there, and Susannah's on the way."

I kept my tone casual, though anticipation flared inside. "See you there."

The moment I was in my truck and had started the engine, I grinned. I might not want to ponder it, but I was worried Lucy would find a way to avoid me. She wouldn't be able to tonight.

Chapter Fourteen

LUCY

I leaned back in my chair, glancing around Wildlands. Wildlands Bar and Lodge was a favorite for locals and tourists. It was situated on the shores of Swan Lake, the centerpiece of Willow Brook. With its prime location, the lodge ran its own floatplane services, carrying tourists out in an array all across the wilderness of Alaska. Hunters, hikers, fishermen, sightseers, eco-tourists and more came here to stay and take off for distant parts. Wildlands Bar was busy all year, and tonight was no exception. Susannah and I had arrived before the rest of our friends and snagged a table right by the windows.

While Susannah took a call on her phone, I looked out over Swan Lake. Like most of

Alaska, the view was spectacular. The lake's far shore was roughly a half a mile across. Birch and cottonwood mixed with spruce along the shoreline. To one side, it expanded out into an open marshy field. A cluster of moose stood in the field this evening, nibbling on alder trees. To the other side, the trees thickened into mostly spruce forest, which stretched into the foothills of the Alaska Range.

Long, slow sunsets were typical during summers in Alaska. Tonight, the sky was a watercolor of pinks, purples, and soft rays of silvery gold. The sun was a disappearing orange ball in the sky, merely its upper curve still visible above the horizon. Opposite the sun, the moon rose, a half crescent in the wispy light of dusk. A flock of Trumpeter swans floated in the lake. They were the namesakes for this lake. The elegant swans floated through the pink light cast across the lake.

The hum of a floatplane sounded in the distance as it approached the lake. I watched as it came to a soft landing in the water, leaving ripples across the pond and ruffling the swans as they floated on the surface. I turned back to look at Susannah when she hung up her phone.

"What was that about?" I asked when she glared at the phone as it sat innocuously where she'd set it on the table.

Susannah brushed her strawberry blonde hair back, tucking it behind her ears. She was a hotshot fire fighter, just like Levi. While she was on a different crew, she often helped out with Levi and Cade's crews when needed. This afternoon, all but one of the crews had been dealing with a fire on the outskirts of town. I resisted the urge to ask any questions about Levi. My curiosity about him was a side effect I was coming to find annoying. I didn't like how much he filled my thoughts, yet I couldn't stop thinking about him.

Susannah took a drag on her beer before answering. At a glance, you wouldn't know she was tough as nails. She was fit, strong, and lovely, almost in an endearing way. With her curly strawberry blonde hair, her wide blue eyes and her freckled cheeks, she was quite pretty. Despite her feminine appearance, I'd heard from the guys she was considered one of the most fearless amongst their crews.

After another glare at the phone, she shrugged. "That was Ward."

"Who's Ward?"

"I trained with Ward for my hotshot

training in California," she offered in explanation.

"Okay, so why are you mad at your phone?"

She rolled her eyes. "I don't know why he's calling me. We kinda had a thing."

"What does kinda mean?" I countered.

Susannah's cheeks flushed. "Just that."

"Did you date or something? He obviously means something, or you wouldn't be all cranky just because he called you."

Susannah's glare sharpened to me now. "It was nothing really. Honestly, if I had to give it a label, I would say it was a one night stand. That's it."

"A one night stand isn't nothing. I mean, it's not a big deal, but nothing would be, well, nothing."

That earned me another glare. "Oh, don't you dare give me hell about any guys," she said with a laugh.

"What do you mean?" I asked, trying and failing to keep the defensive edge out of my tone.

Susannah leaned her chin in her hand, narrowing her eyes. "You're kinda anti-men."

Defensiveness rose inside, but I pushed back against it. "I'm not anti-men," I protested.

"So how come you never, ever see anyone?"

I took a long drag from my beer and eyed her. For a flash, I wanted to tell her about Levi, but that would bring a host of questions I was nowhere near ready to answer.

"I'm not anti-men. I just don't date that much," I managed, striving to keep my tone casual. "So why is this guy calling now anyway? When's the last time you talked to him?"

Susannah cocked her head to one side, drumming her fingers on the table. "Not since my training."

"So how long ago was that?"

"Four years," she said simply

"And he's calling now because...?"

Her cheeks flushed, and she lifted her beer, sighing when she discovered it was empty. "Because he just accepted a position here in Willow Brook. On my crew," she added.

"Oh. Well, if that one night stand was nothing, why do you care?"

I wasn't about to say it aloud, but my questions were as much for me as her. As of today, I could say I'd had a one night stand with Levi. I'd spent most of the day mentally arguing with myself over how much it meant.

"Because it might've been the best sex I ever had," she finally said, her flush deepening.

She couldn't have known that one little comment instantly sent my thoughts flashing —again—to last night and this morning with Levi. Both times I'd had sex with Levi had been the best I'd ever had. Just thinking about it now made me hot all over.

"So if it was just a one night stand, did things get weird or...?"

Susannah shook her head. "It happened the night before I moved back here," she explained, leaning back in her chair and signaling at the waitress who was weaving her way through the tables with a tray.

Susannah looked back to me, her brow furrowed with worry. I experienced a pang of empathy, something I likely wouldn't have felt before last night.

"Well, maybe it'll be a good thing for him to move here," I offered.

Susannah's eyes narrowed. "How's it going to be a good thing? It's messy for people on the same crew to get involved with each other. So I just hope..." She paused and waved her hand back-and-forth, searching for her words. "...whatever we had is gone."

"Um, okay..." I began before pausing. Susannah was usually direct and clear. I wasn't accustomed to seeing her be muddled about something, or rather someone, like this. Oddly, it comforted me. When I allowed myself to be honest inside, I could admit I hated, absolutely hated, feeling out of control. Levi definitely made me feel out of control. I gave a mental shake and forced my attention back to Susannah.

"I'm guessing maybe you might still feel something, or you wouldn't be weird about it," I finally offered.

The waitress arrived at our table. Susannah quickly ordered a beer, looking back to me as our waitress hurried away. "Fine, so I'm weird about it, but I haven't seen him in four years so maybe it's nothing. Back to you. You don't worry about guys ever. I actually envy you," she said bluntly.

Tension spooled inside. I'd been tense all day. I couldn't stop thinking about Levi. The glaring problem was I wanted him even more now than I did before. Last night with him had been like pouring a vat of gasoline on the coals of the fire banked between us and lighting them on fire. The burn of that fire was so good and so delicious, I got hot all over just thinking about it. I didn't know how long the fire was going to take to burn out, and I didn't know what to do about any of it.

I hadn't expected to feel this way. I thought it would be just sex. It didn't help at all that sex with Levi was the best sex *ever*. There was something shimmering under the surface with him, something that hit me— smack in the heart. Despite the fact that I could be dismissive about men, I didn't like being that way. I wanted to be more relaxed and, well, normal.

So I met Susannah's gaze. "I'm not anti-men and I do worry about guys. I just don't really talk about them much. I'm really happy for Amelia," I offered, referencing Amelia's personal fairy-tale second chance with Cade. "If Ward moves here and your *best sex ever* becomes more than that, I'll be really happy for you. Hell, if I hadn't believed in happily-ever-after before, Maisie and Beck proved it to the whole wide world. I never expected to see her settle down with anyone, much less Beck."

Susannah flashed a grin. "I know, right? They're perfect together."

As if conjured by name, Amelia and Maisie appeared through the cluster of people crowding the entrance. They threaded their way over to us, slipping into chairs at the table. We'd commandeered a large round table because Susannah anticipated several of the guys from the station would join us. I couldn't help but wonder if Levi would be one of them.

Amelia leaned her elbows on the table with a sigh. "God, I need a drink," she announced.

"Yeah?" I replied, looking her way.

"I haven't even had a chance to tell you because we were at different sites this afternoon. Our new boiler's been back ordered for two more weeks. I love Cade's parents, but I want to be back home."

I should've been frustrated with this news, but I wasn't. Unless I got lucky in the next few weeks, it was going to be at least until October before I could find a rental. Janet had assured me her B&B would have availability then. She even promised me she would let me stay for no charge, so I was prepared to argue that point with her. But that was over six weeks away.

My reaction, or rather lack thereof, confused me. On the one hand, my heart sank and tension coiled inside. Staying with Levi was testing my limits. On the other hand, I wanted to jump up and down for joy. This gave me a perfectly good reason to keep staying with him. That meant I might get more of what I had last night. And that... *That* was fucking crazy.

I realized I hadn't replied while Amelia was looking at me expectantly.

"Well that sucks," I finally offered.

"Gee Lucy, you were totally zoned out there for a minute," Maisie commented with a smile.

Maisie was so cute, it was almost too much. With her round cheeks, her dark curly hair and her wide brown eyes, she was plain adorable. She was pregnant too, which made her even cuter. She'd been so cranky at the station when she first moved to town. She'd gradually become friends with us sometime over the past year. Given how much I understood what it was like to not quite fit in, I'd been happy to see her let down her guard. Beck flat adored her, having gone from the town's playboy to the most loyal fiancé in the world.

He was trying to sweet talk Maisie into having a big wedding, while she was fighting him on it. It wasn't my place to say, but I thought she wasn't used to anybody giving her that much attention. In the end, all that mattered was Beck adored her and he would go along with whatever she wanted. My heart thudded in my chest, emotion knotting in my throat.

Watching my friends fall in love hadn't elicited any contemplation for me personally. Until now. When sex was always ho-hum, I'd figured it wasn't worth the bother to take things further with anyone. Not to mention, letting down my guard made me feel so vulnerable, I could hardly think about it.

Realizing I was spacing out again, I caught Maisie's gaze with a laugh. "Long day. I just spaced out."

Conveniently, our waitress arrived. After taking everyone's orders, she checked to see how many more people are coming.

Amelia glanced to the waitress. "Cade, Beck and Levi will be here. Anybody else?" she asked, flicking her eyes around the table.

"Jesse and maybe Thad, but I'm not sure who else," Maisie added. As the dispatcher at Willow Brook Fire & Rescue, Maisie was the go between for everyone there.

The waitress promised to check back after everyone arrived before she hurried off. Hearing Levi's name had my body tightening in anticipation. I hadn't seen him since this morning, which felt like forever at the moment. Which was, of course, completely ridiculous. Just thinking about him arriving soon had me shifting my legs restlessly as heat coiled in my belly and radiated through my body, swirling into slick need at my core.

I was relieved at the distraction of casual chatter. While Maisie and Amelia debated the finer points of wedding cake, I watched as the last bit of the sun fell below the horizon, its golden rays stretching high into the sky in its wake. I loved living in Willow Brook. In the years since I'd moved here, I'd found my place with friends and work. The spectacular beauty still took my breath away day after day.

I doubted my mother knew it, but her bringing me here after my last stint in foster care had been the best decision for my life. It hadn't even been my decision. In fact, when I'd gone to court that day with my caseworker, I'd been downright pissed off to watch my mom plead with the judge. She'd begged for a chance, promising she'd already left my father. At the time, I'd been positive she was lying. Yet, I'd been wrong. For the first time in my life, she didn't choose him over me.

I was grateful she brought us here, yet there was so much history of being let down, of her cowering in the face of my father and all but once, always choosing him over me. It made it hard to find a way to bridge the chasm between us.

When she walked us out of the courtroom, I'd been given two hours to pack up at my foster home. It hadn't been a great foster home, just okay. All in all, I'd been an easy teenager since all I wanted to do was stay out of the way. I hadn't been thrilled to learn I was leaving town. Before I knew it, we were on a plane flying to Alaska

High school in Willow Brook had been far more bearable than in California. I'd made a few friends. After I graduated and managed to get through college, I started working with Amelia. I finally felt like I'd found my tribe.

I loved my job, I loved my friends, and I felt like I belonged here. My mother was still here, and even now, I kept expecting her to tell me she was going back to my father. We didn't have a great relationship. I would usually find a way to call or visit every few weeks. She actually had a few of her own friends, including Janet. Janet occasionally tried to nudge me into a deeper reconciliation with her. I wasn't there yet.

Right now, looking out over Swan Lake and around at my friends, even with my anxiety gnawing at me inside about seeing Levi, I was happy to be here. Yet, for the first time in years, a thread of regret wove through me. I had easily decided that romance wasn't for me years ago. Maybe some people got lucky in love, but life had taught me plenty about not wishing for too much. The peace and relief of escaping life with my father was profound. Knowing how much he'd torn my mother down to almost nothing had taught me it was best to rely only on myself.

The depth of my physical response to Levi mingling with intimacy was something I hadn't been prepared for. All the more reason to remember why it was smart to avoid emotional entanglements. I didn't need a man, and I certainly didn't need Levi. Lust didn't equate to love. It was nothing more than that.

Chapter Fifteen

LUCY

It wasn't long before the guys arrived at Wildlands, Beck reaching the table first. For a while, Cade had held the honor of the most pussy-whipped man I'd ever known. Beck now held that honor. Beck was ridiculous around Maisie. He consistently embarrassed her with his public displays of affection.

Take now for example. He came up behind her, landed a lingering kiss on her neck before tilting her head back and kissing her as if they were alone in a room. By the time he drew away, Maisie's cheeks were flushed red and her hair tousled.

"Get a room dude," Cade commented with a chuckle as he sat down beside Amelia and dropped a quick kiss on her cheek.

Beck shrugged nonchalantly as he sat down beside Maisie. "I'm just happy to see her, plus you don't have any reason to give me shit. You're as whipped as anybody."

Cade merely shook his head. Our waitress arrived at that moment. Amelia had wisely ordered a pitcher of beer for the guys. While our waitress took a few more orders, I wondered if Levi had changed his plans. It never crossed my mind that I shouldn't be sitting here expecting him to arrive. He hadn't shared his plans with me, but Maisie had seemed to think he'd be here, so I'd hung my silly hopes on that.

Within a few moments, I heard his voice and glanced over my shoulder to see him coming in through the back hallway. His eyes met mine from across the room, darkening the moment our gazes locked. Butterflies amassed in my belly, and I squeezed my thighs together. I needed to get a grip. For God's sake, he was simply walking to the table. I didn't want to embarrass myself, not with all of our friends here. I certainly didn't want it to be obvious something was going on. Levi, easy-going as ever, reached the table and slipped into the only remaining chair. By pure chance, it happened to be beside me.

Over the hum of conversation around us,

he spoke, his voice low and only for my ears. "Hey Lucy, missed you today."

His voice—that honeyed whiskey voice—sent a shiver chasing over my skin. I felt my cheeks heat. "Don't say that," I hissed.

"Why not?" he countered, his mouth curling at the corner in one of those ridiculously sexy grins. His dark blonde hair was damp, so I figured he must've showered at the station.

Calculating that I was better off without steering anywhere near his comment again, I changed the subject quickly. "Were you out at that fire this afternoon?"

"Of course. We got a few new firebreaks established. Looks like the wind is dying down, so we should be able to keep the fire down."

Susannah said something, and Levi looked away, replying to her comment and snagging the pitcher of beer when Cade passed it to him. Nights like this with friends were common. Levi was firmly in the social circle we shared. I knew his history from bits and pieces. He had moved here from Juneau after high school and left later to do his hotshot training in Arizona before returning. His mother was originally from Willow Brook, which was what brought their family back to the area.

On the heels of the intimacy that had passed between us last night, what would normally be a typical evening out with friends didn't feel typical at all. My body was aflame—inside and out. All I could think about was when we could get back to his place, and I could have him all to myself again.

Thinking like that was *so* not me. Fire talk, as Amelia dubbed it, carried on around us. Everybody at the table but Amelia and I worked at the fire station. I half-listened as I sipped at my beer and nibbled on fresh baked bread served for the table. One comment got my ears to perk up.

"You think we'll get called out to that burn outside Fairbanks?" Beck asked.

Levi shrugged beside me before taking a swallow of this beer. "I don't know. We're definitely due for a rotation."

I watched as Maisie's eyes flicked to Beck, concern held there. With Amelia being my best friend and Maisie another close friend, I was accustomed to them worrying about their respective men out in the field. Up until just now, I'd taken that concern at face value. Hotshot firefighters did dangerous work, grueling work that took them away for weeks at a time. It wasn't that I didn't have empathy. I did. It was simply that the worry was usually one step removed from me.

After the closeness I'd felt with Levi, I felt a flicker of apprehension inside. I didn't know where the hell that came from.

Chapter Sixteen

LEVI

The lights caught in the gold of Lucy's hair. With her hair pulled up in a slapdash ponytail, no one could say she was trying to be glamorous. Yet, she was so damn beautiful. I conveniently had a perfect view of the shadowed valley between her breasts. Were I a sane man when it came to her, I'd appreciate the view and nothing more. Yet, I was crazed for her, so it wasn't exactly comfortable to try to relax with friends when I was rock hard.

I was frankly relieved for the hum of conversation around us. Our table of friends was full, and conversation moved along at the usual bantering pace.

I loved that Lucy didn't have a baseball cap on, which was her standard fare. Her ponytail was slightly lopsided with loose ten-drils of her blonde hair framing her face. Her cheeks were flushed as she laughed at some-thing Amelia said. She was slightly tipsy, and I figured I would need to give her a ride.

"Levi!" Jesse Franklin called from across the table.

I glanced over. "Yeah?"

"You must be going deaf. I said your name three times," Jesse offered with a chuckle.

Frankly, I wasn't paying much attention. Lucy's mere existence beside me had mud-dled my brain. Well that, and all the blood had gone straight to my cock. I shrugged and returned his grin. Jesse was one of the guys on my crew, solid, steady and quick with a joke.

"We're betting ahead on the Nenana Ice Classic for next spring," Jesse explained.

"You're betting now? It doesn't even start yet," I replied.

He was referencing an annual ritual where Alaskans bet on when the ice would break on the Nenana River every spring.

Beck caught my eye. "We're having our own pool, so we have to bet early."

"What's the pool so far?"

Cade chuckled, glancing around the table. "Levi doesn't like to bet unless it's worthy."

I rolled my eyes. "So what? I like it to be worth my while."

Jesse chuckled. "Well, the pots already past five hundred from the station."

Beck chimed in. "Last year, Levi wanted the winner to get a flat screen TV."

I felt Lucy's eyes on me and glanced her way, shrugging sheepishly. "My TV broke, so I figured I might as well bargain for something good. Anyway, I'm in. What's the minimum bet?"

"Twenty bucks," Jesse said quickly.

"All right. I'll get it to you tomorrow."

Cade was seated at an angle across from me, his arm slung across Amelia's shoulder. I felt Amelia's curious gaze when I looked her way. Her eyes flicked from me to Lucy, and I wondered if Lucy had said anything to her. I knew they were best friends, yet I didn't know how much Lucy shared when it came to things like that. I ignored Amelia's gaze and listened as Jesse bantered with Beck over when he thought the ice would crack next spring. Lucy murmured something at my side, and I leaned down because I couldn't hear her.

"What's that?" I asked.

Her eyes caught mine, and need bolted through me. My mind suddenly flashed to last night—Lucy's dark blue gaze, hazed with passion and locked to mine as her channel clenched around my cock and she came with a rough, breathy cry.

"Oh, I just said it's silly to bet now. It's not even winter yet," she said with a shrug.

I grinned. "That's what makes it fun. It's totally random. Winning then is even better because you haven't a clue if you might have a chance."

She held my gaze for a beat, and it suddenly felt as if we were talking about something else altogether.

She stared at me, cocking her head to the side. "Really? I like to know," she suddenly said.

"Know what?"

"Well, I like to plan, to make decisions based on contingencies," she explained.

I bit my tongue. I wanted to ask her what kind of contingencies she'd considered when she climbed in my bed last night. But that would definitely piss her off.

Whether Lucy meant it or not, I was busy interpreting every damn thing she said the last few days. She was still a bit of a mystery to me. She'd been standoffish and guarded ever since I'd known her, but then she and Amelia started working together. She slowly got pulled into my social circle. She was a strong woman, her appearance belying her strength—inside and out. Beyond her obvious beauty and the fact that she called to my body in ways too powerful to ignore, half of my attraction to her originally had been the mystery and the challenge.

Last night had only deepened the mystery. She was a passionate woman, that itself didn't surprise me. What startled me was the depth of vulnerability I sensed flickering behind her prickly exterior.

So I listened to her saying that she liked to know things, to plan, to have contingencies, and I filed that away. If I wanted a shot with her...

What the hell was I doing? I didn't usually think about things like this. But then, Lucy was something else.

As I sat there looking at her, it felt as if we were all alone even though we were surrounded by friends, and conversation floated around us. It occurred to me I knew very little about her life beyond the surface.

She moved to Willow Brook in high school and graduated in her senior year. My family had moved here from Juneau right around the same time. I knew her mother in passing, but I certainly didn't know much about her mother. If Lucy had a father who was involved in her life, he sure as hell didn't live here in Willow Brook. Although the town's population exploded every summer with tourists and seasonal residents, the core of locals was tight. You couldn't live here and not eventually be known in passing by everyone else who lived here.

My passing acquaintance with her mother was solely because she was friends with Janet James and my mother. This was the entirety of my knowledge about Lucy beyond her friendship with Amelia and their small circle of friends. I supposed it should give me pause that I was suddenly quite curious about her. I wanted to know why she was so guarded and prickly, why she kept me at a distance, and dammit, I wanted to know why she'd initially rebuffed me so thoroughly.

I'd known what I felt between us. There was a spark, the flame of it flickering higher whenever we were near. Hell, now it was a damn bonfire, but it had always been there. Yet, she hadn't even given me a chance. Until now.

Chapter Seventeen

LEVI

I walked out into the parking lot at Wildlands, looking up toward the night sky. Stars glittered like diamonds with the moon casting a glow over Swan Lake. I felt a tug on my sleeve and glanced over my shoulder to see Amelia.

"Need something?" I asked.

She nodded quickly. "Give Lucy a ride, please."

Lucy had stepped into the restroom in the back hallway as our gathering broke apart.

"Already planning on it," I said in return.

Cade stood beside Amelia, his hand hooked in her back pocket. He caught my eyes as well, nodding in agreement. "Good call. She's had a few too many beers to drive."

"Want me to wait until she comes out?" Amelia asked.

Puzzled, I shrugged. "For what?"

Amelia chewed on the inside of her cheek. "Well, she might argue with you about it," she said with a small smile.

I chuckled. "Oh, I bet she will. I can handle it. You guys go on. I'll catch you tomorrow," I replied, my eyes flicking to Cade.

Amelia looked uncertain, but Cade nodded firmly. "Got it. Come on, babe. Lucy will only get more annoyed if you're here trying to tell her what to do."

Amelia threw a glare at him, but let herself be tugged along. Cade was quite right. Lucy didn't appreciate being told what to do period, much less with an audience.

I watched as they drove away and leaned against the back bumper of Lucy's small truck. I glanced out over Swan Lake, the lights of the lodge reflecting on its still waters. A few more lodges were scattered around the lake's shore, but the far side was empty. The moon cast a shimmering path over the water.

Hearing footsteps, I turned to see Lucy walking from the back door of the lodge. Her eyes narrowed when she saw me leaning against the back of her truck. She stopped a few feet away from me, putting her hands on her hips.

"What are you doing here?" she asked.

"Waiting for you. I'm giving you a ride."

Her eyes narrowed further, her lips tightened, and she shook her head slightly. "I don't need a ride. I wasn't even sure I was coming out to your place anyway."

No surprise there. I didn't say my thoughts aloud. I cocked my head to the side and held her gaze. "And where were you planning to stay then?"

She shrugged.

"Well, you're in no shape to drive."

"I'm not drunk," she protested. "I only had three beers."

"You weigh next to nothing."

"I do not! In fact, I weigh almost one-hundred and fifteen pounds" Her speech wasn't quite slurred, but it was close.

I bit back the urge to laugh because that most definitely wouldn't help matters.

"Amelia asked me to give you a ride," I offered.

Lucy tapped her foot, her glare becoming more mutinous.

"Amelia is not my keeper," she mumbled.

"No, she's your friend. She asked me to give you a ride, but I was already planning on it. You're not driving anywhere. In fact, I'm not getting off the back of your truck until you hand over your keys."

Lucy pulled her phone, or rather attempted to pull her phone, out of her pocket. It clattered to the ground. She leaned over to pick it up, her aim only slightly off when she stumbled. I snagged it quickly, only to have her stumble into me. When her shoulder bumped into mine, I steadied her.

She snatched the phone out of my hand. "I'm calling Amelia," she announced as she quickly tapped her screen and called Amelia, on speaker no less.

Amelia answered immediately. "Hey Lucy, what's up? Are you arguing with Levi about giving you a ride?"

I chuckled. "Yes, she is," I said.

Amelia didn't even laugh. "Lucy, don't be stupid. Just let Levi give you a ride. You're staying with him anyway, so it's not like it's out of his way."

"What if I don't want to stay with him?"

Amelia didn't miss a beat. "You're welcome to come to Cade's parents, but it seems kind of silly. If you try to drive over here, I'm going to tell Levi not to let you. Cade and I will come back to pick you up. How's that?"

I was starting to realize Lucy might be drunker than I'd initially thought. She bit her lip, glaring at her phone. "I can't stay at Levi's anymore," she said, her words definitely slurring now.

"How come?" Amelia asked.

"Because we had sex!" Lucy announced.

My mouth dropped open, part of a laugh escaping before I cut if off. She'd shocked the hell out of me.

I could practically imagine the look on Amelia's face about now. She was silent when the sound of the car's blinker echoed through the line. At which point, I realized Lucy had just made her announcement on the car's speakerphone.

"Are we on speakerphone?" I asked.

"Sure are," Cade offered, his smile evident in his tone.

Lucy's eyes flicked up to mine, wide and almost panicked. "I was joking, just joking."

Another long silence ensued.

There was no way in hell I was going to add anything at this point.

Lucy sighed. "I'll let Levi drive me home. Okay, bye."

She ended the call without waiting for

Amelia or Cade to say goodbye, dropping the phone in the process. I picked it up, only to realize she hadn't managed to end the call. "Guys, I got it. I'm driving. Talk to you tomorrow."

"Night Lucy. Thanks Levi," Amelia said quickly over Cade's low laugh.

I successfully tapped the *end call* button and handed the phone back to Lucy.

We stared at each other in the cool evening air, the sounds from the bar drifting out over the lake. After a beat, she opened her mouth and then snapped it shut. She crossed her arms across her chest, her cheeks flushing slightly.

"Oh my God. That was dumb," she announced, almost as if she were talking to herself. She took a ragged breath and looked away. "I can't believe this." Her eyes swung back to me. "I hate this," she muttered.

"Hate what?"

"This... this thing with us. I hate that I want you. It's annoying and stupid and you make me crazy. The good kind of crazy and the bad kind."

Ah, so we were back to how much she hated the fact we had some serious chemistry. I knew there was no great way to resolve that, so I elected to address the part I could.

"It's no big deal. You have the perfect excuse. You can say you were drunk and joking. If you want, I'll tell Amelia there's no way in hell we had sex. Just tell me what to do."

As she stared at me, I saw the barest hint of vulnerability flickering in her gaze. I wanted her. Badly. I couldn't say how it had come to this point so swiftly, but everything just felt right with her.

My father had always told me I would know when it was the right woman. Back when I was a teenager and didn't give a damn, all I wanted was sex. My father made a point of letting me know that having fun was perfectly fine, but to always treat women with respect. Yet, he'd insisted someday I'd come across the right woman, and I would know. Back then, I'd dismissed him as a silly romantic.

My father adored my mother and insisted their marriage was one for the ages—his words, not mine. He doted on her to the point I'd thought he was ridiculous when I was younger. My mother was a strong willed, independent woman, but she adored him too.

As I stared back at Lucy, for the first time, I considered that perhaps my father wasn't crazy. There was just something about her. Hell if I knew why. I could easily explain my attraction to her. She took my breath away. Yet, she was guarded, prickly and a challenge the likes I'd never considered worth it. With her though, I didn't even think twice about the effort.

Between my initial chasing after her and getting shot down and then last night, I knew there was something there, something I hadn't felt with anyone. I wanted to wall away the world and tell her not to worry. Because she always seemed worried, as if she was ready to fight the world, whether the fight was necessary or not. I wanted to wrap her in my arms and tell her to let go, to simply forget the rest of the world with me. Yet, I didn't dare. Not now. I knew if I pushed too far, too fast, she'd shut me out.

In that vein, I would happily lie for her about the fact we were burning the sheets up. I would wait until she was comfortable before staking my claim publicly. She surprised me though.

After studying me for a moment, she shook her head sharply. "No, that's stupid. Amelia knows me too well. I don't know why I went and said that, but I can face the music." She sighed, her shoulders curling in. "I guess you have to give me a ride now."

"I was already giving you a ride, Lucy," I said, softening my tone. "Not because I'm bossing you around and telling you what to do, but because I'd give any friend who might've had a few too many beers a ride home. Well, that and Amelia would kick my ass if I didn't."

A soft smile claimed her lips as she nodded. "We can't have that. She could take you too."

I chuckled, pushing off the back of her truck. Lucy turned and started walking across the parking lot.

I called out, "Need anything from your truck?"

"Nope!"

Her voice lilted with the word, carrying to me and winding its way around my heart. Fuck. She'd barreled straight into my heart. I needed to play this hand just right, or she'd run so far and so fast, I'd never catch her.

I jogged to catch up and reached my truck first, opening the passenger door for her. She climbed in quickly and leaned her head back with a sigh. She was quiet on the drive home through the darkness. When I pulled up at my house, I glanced over to see she was sound asleep.

Her face was relaxed in sleep, the moonlight limning her features. One hand was curled against her chin, while the other—still in its brace—rested on her lap. My heart clenched. I climbed out quietly, hoping I didn't wake her when I shut the door gently. Rounding the truck, I found her still sound asleep when I opened the passenger door. Bundling her against me, I carried her inside.

She was warm and relaxed in my arms as I carefully closed the door with my boot. Walking upstairs, Ham came scurrying over, sniffing at my feet and looking up at Lucy.

"Hey Ham, how ya been?" I whispered.

After another sniff, Ham meandered away and leapt on a shelf by the window where I kept one of the wheels he liked to run on. He climbed into a little nest of fabric there and settled in to look out into the darkness.

I paused, considering whether I should take Lucy to the guest bedroom or mine. To be honest, I didn't ponder this long and quickly carried her into my bedroom, if only because I wanted to fall sleep beside her again.

I took off her boots and jeans and somehow even managed to get her bra off.

After tucking her under the covers in her t-shirt and underwear, I quickly stripped down to my briefs and climbed in beside her. She was still asleep, her breathing steady and even. On the heels of a soft exhalation, she draped herself against me, hooking one of her knees over my legs and burrowing her head against my shoulder.

With her warm, lush body curled against mine, I drifted into sleep, contemplating it would be perfectly fine, hell it would be far better than fine, to fall sleep like this with her every night.

Chapter Eighteen

LUCY

I came awake slowly. Levi's bedroom was dark, save the soft glow from the night light beside the bed. He was curled up behind me. I was so warm and relaxed, I couldn't help but savor how protected I felt wrapped tight in his embrace.

I could feel his arousal pressing against my bottom and the slick heat between my thighs. It didn't seem to matter whether I was awake or asleep, my body responded to him. I wanted him. Badly.

As if to illustrate the point, without my brain even forming a thought, I shifted my hips, pressing back into the hard, hot length of his cock. I almost moaned aloud.

There were fuzzy fragments of the sleepy

memory of him carrying me inside, but I didn't remember him undressing me.

My thoughts were hazy, sleepy, and soaked with desire. Too many nights of waking up yearning for him without having him near me were only exacerbated by his willing body curled up behind me.

When I wiggled my hips again, I felt his body come awake with a subtle hum of tension. His palm was resting on my belly, warm against my skin. His touch slid up to cup one of my breasts, his thumb teasing my nipple.

I shifted my legs restlessly, the need contained in my core building. It was as if we'd already had hours of foreplay when we'd simply been sleeping.

Levi murmured something into my hair and then shifted, removing his hand from my breast and out from under my shirt. Brushing my tangled hair away from my neck, he dusted kisses there. I didn't know what was worse, the fact that I moaned instantly and my skin prickled in the wake of his touch. Or the fact that I was almost bereft with disappointment to have his touch abandon my breast.

Another moan escaped as his teeth closed softly on the sensitive skin just behind my ear. His hand got busy again pushing my shirt up to tease my nipples, all the while his hips rocked, his cock pressing into the cleft of my bottom.

I reached between us with my good hand, curling my palm over his cock through the thin cotton of his briefs. He growled my name into my neck, sending a wash of goose bumps over my entire body. Heat spun wildly in my belly, radiating outward as pleasure scored through me. I was torn. I wanted everything all at once. I didn't want him to stop touching me anywhere. His touch, sure and stealthy, slid down over my belly and into my panties, his fingers dipping into the slick heat there. I was drenched, so wet his fingers slid in easily as my hips bucked into his touch.

He drove his fingers into me deeply, first one and then another, stretching my channel and making me nearly frantic for more. His name fell from my lips with a gasp and a cry. Need coiled so tightly inside, I didn't want to wait. Then he was shoving my panties down my legs, and I kicked them loose under the covers.

I felt him roll away from me. My body was like a seeking missile, instantly following his.

"Where are you going?" I asked, my voice breathy and demanding at once.

Perhaps a second passed before he was rolling back to me, and I heard the sound of foil tearing. I felt the hot velvety skin of his cock pressing against my bare bottom as he shimmied out of his briefs.

He rolled a condom on and reached between us, the calloused surface of his palm caressing my bottom. He murmured my name as he slid his cock between my thighs. He teased me, dragging the thick head of his cock back and forth between my slick folds, coasting over my clit.

All the while, he made me wild with need. I was so wet, juices from my desire were coating the insides of my thighs. I didn't care that I was murmuring, gasping, crying out and calling his name.

"Stop torturing me," I choked out.

With a soft chuckle, he finally sank inside of me in one slow slide. He held still for a beat, rocking his hips and seating himself deeply. My channel throbbed around him. It felt so good to have him filling me, I sighed in relief and pleasure.

Levi brushed my hair back again, tracing my brows. As he trailed his fingertip down my cheek, his touch feather light, his teeth closed down on the side of my neck, just sharp enough to make me cry out. When his finger traced my lips, I caught it in my teeth, drawing it in, swirling my tongue around it and mimicking his motion as he drew back and sank into my pussy again.

There was spooning, and then there was this—Levi curled up tight behind me, his cock buried deeply inside as we slowly rocked together. He drew his finger free of my mouth, his wet touch trailing down to tease my nipples and pinching them lightly. I was so close to the edge, my pussy soaking wet as he drew back and sank inside with nothing more than a subtle adjustment of his hips. Pleasure tightened inside of me. His touch, strong and knowing, slid down over my belly, into my curls and pressed over my clit.

Pleasure unspooled in slow motion inside of me, rolling through me in wave after wave, rocking me to my very bones. I was crying out, incoherent as I gasped his name and my pussy clamped down on his cock. I felt his release as his cock pulsed inside of me.

We stilled together. His hand slid up to rest on my belly as our breath slowed. I relaxed in his embrace, feeling better than I could remember ever feeling in the middle of the night—utterly and completely satiated.

Warm, safe, and protected. It distantly occurred to me I should be worried, but I felt
too good to care.

In the darkness, I could feel his heart
pounding against my back, its beat strong
and sure. He drew away, just long enough to
dispose of his condom before returning.

"Lucy?" he asked, his voice husky.

"Mmm, hmm?"

"I didn't expect this," he said gruffly.

I didn't know how to respond to that. I
held still and then surprised myself with my
own words.

"I know. Me neither."

I fell asleep with him curled up behind
me, holding me close.

Chapter Nineteen

LUCY

I sat at a small round table in Firehouse Café, nibbling on one of Janet's delicious wild blueberry scones. I tried and failed to keep my mind occupied by staring out the window. With Firehouse Café situated smack in the middle of downtown Willow Brook on Main Street, there were plenty of people to watch. At the moment, two teenage siblings were arguing over who was riding in the front seat while their mother ignored them as she loaded up luggage into the back of the hatchback.

Despite this potential distraction, my thoughts were churning and had been all morning. Amelia was meeting me here, and I was mortified in anticipation of seeing her. I still couldn't quite believe I'd announced Levi and I had sex to her and Cade last night. Just thinking about it now, my cheeks heated.

Janet slipped into the chair across from me at the table, handing me my coffee.

"Morning dear. You look, I dunno, a little off this morning. You doing okay?" she asked.

Janet's warm brown eyes held a hint of concern. With flour dusted on her apron, her silver hair pulled atop her head with a pencil, she evinced an air of warmth. Not to mention, she always smelled good simply because she was a phenomenal baker and carried the scent of sugar and cinnamon with her.

I shrugged. "I was out late last night, that's all."

I sure as hell wasn't about to announce to her what was really going on, namely I was screwing Levi and couldn't seem to keep my hands off of him. I could barely even think about last night. It wasn't the getting tipsy and blurting out that I had sex with him to Amelia and Cade on speakerphone, it wasn't that Levi carried me to his bed, and I didn't remember getting there. None of these things were weighing on me beyond minor embarrassment.

Rather, what was weighing on me was all about how I felt when I was with Levi. My mind spun back to last night—to waking up with him curled around me, his arousal pressing against my bottom with me already soaked with need. Our encounter had been this sleepy, hot, dreamy sex. It had been so slow, deep, and intense, I blushed even thinking about it now. My orgasm had started at my toes and rolled through me, shattering me at my core. I could still feel myself falling back to sleep with him curled up tight against me and his lips on my neck.

I didn't know how long we slept after that because I had no idea what time it was. I came awake when I heard his on-call pager beeping on the nightstand by the bed. He'd dropped a kiss on my neck and reluctantly drawn away. I'd instantly ached for his presence and climbed out of bed to make him coffee. With Ham following me curiously down the stairs, I'd fed him first with some lettuce and carrots before starting a pot of coffee.

When Levi walked into the kitchen a few minutes later, the smile that claimed his lips gave my heart a swift kick.

Janet cleared her throat, rather audibly, effectively nudging me out of my reverie. I was all kinds of out of sorts this morning. I took a gulp of my coffee, lifting my mug in gratitude. "Delicious, as always."

Janet merely nodded. "Seen your mom lately?"

"Couple of weeks ago," I offered. I wasn't sure how much Janet really knew about what had gone down with my family before my mom and I moved here. I was glad Janet was friends with my mom, but I wasn't sure what she expected of us.

I surprised myself with my question. "What do you ask about my mom for? You see her more than me probably."

It was hard to surprise Janet, but this did the trick. Her eyes widened slightly, yet she didn't miss a beat. She cocked her head to the side. "I love you hon, and I love your mom. I hope maybe you two could get past everything that happened before you moved here."

Ah, so perhaps my mother had given a few clues. "Look, we're at peace. I'm not walking around holding a grudge. We're just not that close. Things were really, well, shitty with my dad. I don't know how much she's told you about that."

"Hon, I think she's told me everything. Let me give you the short version. Your dad beat the shit out of her sometimes, he was emotionally abusive, and he ignored you. She shoulda left when you were a little girl, and she didn't. He finally beat the shit out of you one day, and she lost you because she couldn't make the right decision at the time. The way she tells it, she didn't have the strength. I'm not saying that's right, but it is what it is. By the time she found the strength to leave, she was afraid it was too late."

I stared at Janet, my heart feeling funny in my chest. She wasn't saying anything I didn't already know. Yet, hearing it spelled out so succinctly and knowing my mother had spoken this directly about it made me sad. I was okay. I really was. I had moved on and scabbed over the scrapes and bumps my childhood had left on me.

Honestly, my childhood wasn't something I dwelled on, probably because it always hurt a little. I had enough sense to know I couldn't change the past, so I simply tried to accept it. Not certain what to say to Janet, I simply nodded and took another swallow of my coffee.

"I'm glad she has a friend like you," I finally said.

Janet reached across the table to squeeze my hand before standing and adjusting her apron. "I wasn't trying to pry. Just letting you know she doesn't expect anything from you.

Maybe it will help you to know she understands where you're coming from."

With a warm smile, she changed the subject. "Amelia meeting you here soon?"

"Yep, I'm sure she'll be here any minute."

As if conjured by name, the bell jingled over the café door, and I glanced over to see Amelia entering. She gave a wave and strode up to the counter. Janet squeezed my shoulder and hurried over. I returned to nibbling on my scone.

Within moments, Amelia walked over, shrugging her jacket off as she slipped into the chair across from me. I took a fortifying gulp of coffee, figuring I'd best cut to the chase.

"So I was a little tipsy last night when I said that, but it's true," I said flatly.

Amelia's eyes narrowed, and I saw a hint of mirth in them. "It doesn't surprise me."

My cheeks got hot. I was embarrassed, but it would pass. Amelia might tease me, but I knew that would be all it was. I rolled my eyes. "Why doesn't it surprise you?"

"Because he's had a thing for you forever, and it's obvious you like him too."

My mouth dropped open. "What?! How is that obvious?"

Amelia grinned. "You two are like kids.

He teases you, and you get all bitchy. It's not like other guys haven't tried to get you to go out with them, but only Levi gets under your skin. Let's face it, he's handsome as hell. He's not for me, but you can't deny it," she said with a laugh.

I smiled even though I didn't want to. "Fine. So he's handsome. I'm not serious relationship material," I said flatly, ignoring the funny little thump of my heart.

"Why are we talking about getting serious already?" she asked. "You don't have to skip to that right off. A little fun wouldn't hurt you. To be honest, I'm not one to talk up one night stands, but you are way overdue to get laid and have been for too damn long. I mean, when's the last...?"

My cheeks were so hot I needed a fan. "Oh my God. Shut the hell up. You know I hardly ever date. My vibrator is as good as any guy."

The moment I said that, for the first time ever, I was lying. Levi was far and away better than my vibrator, but I wasn't about to fess up to that just now.

"Bullshit," she said bluntly. "You definitely don't date, but good sex is better than a vibrator any day."

She took a sip of her coffee and broke off the

end of my scone when I pushed the plate in her direction. "Look, you're awesome and Levi's a good guy. I can't even say he's a player. He dates here and there that's pretty much it. Why not relax and enjoy some fun for once in your life?"

"I have fun!"

Amelia shook her head. "I know you do. Not with guys though."

I sighed, ceding this argument. It wasn't worth it, not just now. "I have to find another place to stay."

"Well, you'd better get on it then," she said with a wry grin. "Unless you want to come stay with Cade's parents, I'm not sure how much luck you'll have right now. I'd offer our place, but the downstairs floor is torn up, and we have no hot water."

"I don't want to stay with Cade's parents. That'll be weird because it makes it seem like I'm like too childish to stay with Levi."

"Aren't you then?" Amelia countered.

I resisted the urge to throw the last bite of my scone at her and satisfied myself with a glare.

"You could always call your mom," she added, her tone softening.

What was it with people bringing up my mom today? I sighed and shook my head softly. "No, that would be even weirder. Janet already gave me a little pep talk about her today."

Amelia held my gaze evenly. She was one of the few people that I'd confided in about my life before Willow Brook. "Well, then I say you keep staying at Levi's and maybe have lots more sex."

I burst out laughing, my cheeks heating even more. "Oh my God! Don't even, okay? It's bad enough that Cade heard."

"I felt terrible last night. Seriously. As soon as you made your little announcement, I knew you were gonna die when you realized you were on speakerphone. If you'd told me sooner, I could've headed you off," she said bluntly.

"It was just the night before," I mumbled. "I really wasn't holding out on you."

"Like I said, Levi's a good guy. He's close to his sister, and his parents are great. Honestly, if you were looking for something more than sex, he's a pretty good candidate," she said.

My heart tumbled in my chest, and I felt as if I was falling inside—that feeling you get when an elevator goes down too fast and your whole stomach drops with it. Or when you're on a roller coaster and it rounds the top of a curve before plummeting down.

None of this was supposed to happen. I wasn't supposed to want Levi so much it made me ache. I wasn't supposed to give into it and then feel as if I were being bound in a web of intimacy that felt so good it terrified me.

I mistakenly assumed my first thought had been unspoken, but Amelia's eyes widened.

"Oh my God. What did I just say out loud?"

"That it wasn't supposed to happen," she said calmly before taking a sip of coffee. Setting her mug down, she eyed me. "Try to relax and maybe enjoy it. You know I'm here for you. No judgment. Ever."

My throat tightened because I knew she meant it. She was loyal to the bone and there for me no matter what.

"I know," I finally said, quickly shifting topics. "I suppose we should get to work, huh?"

Amelia shrugged. "Don't you have a doctor's appointment soon?" she asked, her eyes flicking to the brace on my forearm.

"Next week. She said I should be good to go by then."

"Good. There's plenty to do no matter

what. We're due to start the tile cutting for the bathrooms. You can do that, and I'll do all the heavy labor," she offered with a grin.

"You love this, don't you? You get to insist I do all the boring, tedious shit."

She burst out laughing. "I don't love it, but it's good for you to take it easy and to maybe accept a little help here and there."

I rolled my eyes as I stood. "I don't need anyone's help," I muttered as I snagged my empty coffee mug and plate.

Chapter Twenty

LEVI

Pulling my fire gloves off my hands as I stepped away from a firebreak we'd been working on, I spun around to scan the horizon. Smoke hazed the sky in this section of the forest, although the wind had finally slowed, so it was thinning out. I dragged my sleeve across my face and rested a hand on my hip as I caught my breath. The same fire we'd dealt with last week in a section of forest outside Willow Brook had kicked up again yesterday. It had originally been sparked earlier this summer after some campers ignored the no campfire rule. We'd largely contained it, but too many days of dry weather and wind kept fanning the flames.

We'd spent most of the day creating several new firebreaks on the outskirts of the area to help keep the fire from spreading if the wind changed direction. Though there were postings everywhere about the campfire ban, the wilderness in Alaska—even in areas with nearby towns—wasn't like the manicured trails in the Lower 48. Hikers and campers often lost track of where they were, or didn't take certain restrictions seriously. With a dry summer, we had to monitor for wildfires all season long.

I glanced over at Jesse Franklin as he approached. He set the chainsaw he'd been using down nearby and caught my eye.

"Think we're done for the day?" he asked.

I nodded, leaning over to snag a water bottle on the ground. I took a long draw from it, wiping my mouth with my sleeve. "Damn good the wind died down this afternoon, and we had a chance to do this."

"Too much dead spruce around here," he added.

The forest had started to recover from the spruce bark beetles, which had decimated entire swaths of this area a while back. Even though there was new growth, it would be another few decades before the forest recovered.

"Yeah, we'll post some more signs later this week, especially in the busier areas. That should hopefully prevent another entirely unnecessary fire."

Jesse nodded and spun to scan the horizon, replying to something another crewmember approaching us said.

Cade's crew was out here with us as well. For a few years, I was a foreman on his crew, but I'd taken over as superintendent for another crew last year. I'd barely spoken to Cade today, if only because we were working hard. Even in downtimes when we weren't actively fighting a fire, hotshot firefighting was damn hard work. Today had been filled with hours of clearing trees, downing dead ones and creating firebreaks along streams, using the landscape to our advantage.

I spun around, looking in the distance as the smoke cleared. Denali was visible through the haze, rising tall in the sky. Denali was the tallest mountain peak in North America. All of the central towns in Alaska were within view of Denali. I took a deep breath and let it out as my eyes traveled away from Denali through fields of fireweed, a bright fuchsia weed dotting the Alaskan landscape in the open areas.

A ribbon of river wound through a valley,

leading to Willow Brook. The river in question was our town's namesake, laughingly called a brook. It was wide and shallow, and ran down from the mountains, feeding into Swan Lake.

My mind spun to Lucy. She'd become the touchstone for my thoughts at all times lately. She'd insisted this morning that she didn't care to try to gloss over her tipsy announcement to Amelia and Cade last night. I knew how private she was, so I knew she wasn't enjoying the spot she'd put herself in. Yet, it was so like her to insist on facing it head on. I loved how she never backed down from anything. That look of vulnerability had flickered in her eyes. Just thinking about it now, my heart squeezed again. I had stared into her gorgeous blue eyes and considered that I'd happily cart her back to bed and stay there all day.

"Let me handle it, but do me a favor and don't take this as permission to announce it to the world," she'd said.

"Hey, I wouldn't have said a damn thing," I'd countered with a wink.

"I was a little tipsy," she'd replied, a slow smile claiming her lips.

I'd grinned, relieved she wasn't cranky about the whole thing. We didn't speak of what passed during the night. The moment her bottom wiggled against my cock, I'd come out of my half sleep, already rock hard and ready. It seemed as though we weren't going to talk about the fact we couldn't keep our hands off of each other.

I supposed we didn't have to talk about it. I knew I needed to wait and bide my time. Because if there was one thing I knew about Lucy, she did *not* like to be pressured into anything.

———

Later that afternoon, I leaned my head against the wall behind me on a bench in our locker room. At the sound of footsteps, I glanced up to see Cade approaching. He sat down across from me.

"So any comment on that little convo last night?" he asked, the hint of a grin tugging at the corners of his mouth.

I shrugged. "Nothing to add," I offered.

He held my gaze for a moment and then nodded. "Wasn't trying to gossip. If you need someone to talk to, I'm here."

I leaned my elbows on my knees. "Why would you think I needed to talk?"

He was quiet for a beat. "Seems to me

you kinda have a thing for Lucy. Have for a while."

It was easy to forget how perceptive Cade was. I'd known him for years. He tended to be low-key and quiet. Damn if he hadn't honed in on exactly what was going on with me. What I had for Lucy was a hell of a lot more than a *thing* though. Problem was I had to be patient. I sure as hell knew she would *not* appreciate anything even remotely resembling gossip about us. But Cade wasn't one to gossip.

So, I held his gaze and nodded slowly. "You might say that. I know you won't talk but I'm gonna have to ask you not to say a damn thing. Lucy will tear me a new one if she thinks anyone more than you two hears about us."

He chuckled. "Oh, I know. Amelia figured Lucy was pretty upset about saying anything last night. You know you don't have to worry about us."

"I know." I paused, chewing on my thoughts. "Look, Lucy'll run for the hills if she gets wind I might be hoping for more than a little fun between the sheets."

Cade was quiet before his grin stretched slowly across his face. "That she will. You'd best know what you want."

"I do," I said, my heart giving a hard thump as I spoke.

"Hey guys, what are we dealing with now?" Beck asked as he rounded the corner into the locker room.

Beck's crew was picking up where we left off this afternoon out at the fire site. He slid onto the bench across from me and glanced between Cade and I.

Cade replied first. "We established the perimeter on the far side of that tricky ravine and by the river. If you guys take care of the opposite side, we should be good.

"Anything else my guys should know?" Beck asked.

"Don't think so. The wind died down, so the fire's not spreading anymore. Fred's doing a flyover to check the perimeters," I offered, referencing one of our local pilots who often helped fly our crews out to fires.

Beck stood. "Got it."

My cell phone rang, and I slipped it from my front pocket, glancing down to see my dad's name flash on the screen. "Gotta take this guys," I said as I stood and stepped away.

"Hey Dad, what's up?" I asked.

"Hey son, could use a little help this afternoon if you've got a few minutes," he replied quickly.

"Just finishing up at the station. Whaddya need?"

"Looks like some rain might be rolling in tonight, and I need a little help getting the firewood we had delivered put away."

"Sure I'll be by. Give me a half hour or so, okay?"

I left the station wondering if I should let Lucy know I would be home later than usual. I laughed to myself. Before a few days ago, I wouldn't. She was so insistent that I just live the way I would normally even though she was staying with me. Yet, if any other friend were staying with me, I'd likely let them know. It was simple courtesy.

Yet, now that I'd been buried deep inside of her, as close as we could physically be, every simple action felt loaded. I knew my parents would offer me dinner. The natural extension of that circumstance would be Lucy eating canned soup. Because she did *not* cook. I'd noticed that unless I cooked something, she grabbed whatever easy thing she could. I contemplated inviting her to my parents, yet I didn't know how much she'd read into that.

I didn't let myself think too much. Before driving out of the parking lot, I texted her quickly.

Chapter Twenty-One

LUCY

My phone vibrated on the dresser. I'd just fin-ished taking a shower and was tugging a sweatshirt over my head. It was chilly out this late afternoon. After a clear, calm day, clouds had rolled in, bringing a chill along with them.

I yanked my sweatshirt down and strolled to the dresser to glance at my phone screen. Tapping it, I saw a text from Levi.

I'm helping my dad stack some wood, and my mom's cooking. I thought you might want to stop by. You're welcome of course. My mom's a better cook than me. ;)

I stuffed my hands in the front pocket of my sweatshirt and stared down at my phone —as if though the phone itself was a person standing in front of me. I chewed the inside of my cheek and turned away, walking to look out the windows. Though it was gray outside, the view from the guest bedroom was a splash of color. The window looked out over a field of fireweed. The fuchsia stood out even more brightly amidst the drab landscape this late afternoon.

My heart was pounding hard and fast, and I didn't know why. It shouldn't make me nervous to have dinner with Levi and his parents. It was something any of my close friends here would do. I'd had dinner with Amelia and her parents, along with Cade's family and Susannah's. Yet, I'd never felt the way I did about Levi. He'd moved from the category of casual friend who sort of annoyed me to far more. As such, his casual invitation somehow felt loaded.

I felt silly and sheepish though. If I stayed here, I'd probably have soup for dinner. I had complete faith that Levi's mother was an amazing cook, if only because he was and he insisted it was all because of her. It would be nice not to be alone with my thoughts. I couldn't decide if it would send a message if I went, or more of a message if I didn't.

Oh my God. You need to calm the fuck down.

You're making this way more than it is. Just like Amelia said, you can have a little fun. It doesn't have to be anything else.

I shook my critical thoughts away. Spinning away from the windows, I snagged my phone off the dresser, typing out my reply before I thought too much harder.

Thanks. Sounds great. You know I'll probably just have soup if I stay here anyway.

As soon as I set the phone down, it occurred to me I had no idea where his parents lived. Feeling sheepish, I grabbed my phone again.

Where and when?

His reply was swift.

Cottonwood Hollow, last house on the road. A big yellow farmhouse looking place. Come anytime. I'm on my way there now. Scratch that. Don't come early because I know you'll end up trying to help. How's your arm anyway?

Warmth swirled in my belly and curled up around my heart. I shouldn't savor it so much to have him be concerned, but I did. I glanced down at the brace on my wrist. I hadn't experienced pain in days now and was about ready to say screw it. The only thing stopping me was I knew Amelia would get on my case. So would Levi. I flushed straight through at that thought. Because he would, and what that said about him and how much a part of me savored the fact he cared enough to nag was almost too much for me to contemplate.

It's fine. I'll be there soon. I have one good hand. I can help.

His reply was almost instantaneous.

Trying to win an award for being stubborn? No way in hell I'm letting you stack wood with one hand. Don't fight me on this. You can hang with my mom in the kitchen. She'll love it.

My heart did another tumble in my chest, and my throat tightened with emotion.

Chapter Twenty-Two

LUCY

The cool metal of my silver bracelet slid through my fingers as I sat at the kitchen table in Levi's parents' house. Levi's mother, Gloria, was chopping onions and chatting away while she did so. I'd offered to help but she declined, insisting she was too bossy in her own kitchen.

I was restlessly fiddling with my bracelet because I was anxious. I was fielding a host of new feelings. I'd never had enough of a relationship with any man to meet his family. I didn't know what to call what Levi and I were doing, yet somehow it didn't sit right to pass it off as some sort of friends with benefits thing. So, that was confusing to me. Then, there was the odd feeling of wanting his mother to like me. I'd never cared much about anything like that. At the moment, I was trying to hold all of my internal unrest at bay and staring idly out the window. Gloria's voice nudged me back into awareness.

"Lucy?" she asked.

"Oh, I'm sorry. I was enjoying your view," I explained.

Their home was in a lovely area at the end of a road just beyond downtown Willow Brook. There was a narrow stream running along the edge of a field to the side of their home with trees in the distance and the peak of Denali visible above the tree line. The field was awash in color from the fireweed and lupine, bright amidst the misty rain falling outside.

Gloria cast a smile in my direction as she paused in her chopping to turn on a burner. Levi had inherited his rich blue eyes from his mother, along with his dark gold hair. Hers was pulled up atop her head with a chopstick as she moved about the kitchen.

Quickly pouring olive oil in the pan, she added the chopped onions to it and gave them a quick stir. The kitchen was large and airy with a picture window looking out over the view. A round table was situated in front of the window. An island served as a divider between the dining area and working area. It was clear that the kitchen was the center of this household.

Gloria had taken me on a tour of the house when I arrived, shooing Levi back outside to help his father chop and stack wood. I'd been briefly introduced to his father, Brad Phillips. His father had a quick smile, blue eyes and dark brown hair.

Their home had a large living room just across the hallway from the kitchen. A staircase in the center led up to a hallway with doors to four bedrooms. After the quick tour, Gloria had escorted me into the kitchen where she plied me with wine. I'd been happy for it, anything to take the edge off of my frayed nerves.

"It is a lovely view," isn't it?" she commented.

"Oh yes. But then it's hard not to find a lovely view around here," I replied with a little laugh.

Gloria chuckled. "So true. Where do you live?"

A perfectly innocent question. Normally, I wouldn't think twice about sharing that I was staying with Levi. Yet, it felt funny because the last three nights had demonstrated beyond any doubt that I wasn't simply staying with Levi as a friendly houseguest. Rather, I'd been as intimate as it was physically possible to be with him. The flush started at my toes, sending tingles through my body. I took a gulp of wine and tried to keep a straight face.

"Oh, I'm between apartments right now. Levi was nice enough let me stay at his place for the time being. I think he took pity on me and invited me for dinner tonight because I'm a terrible cook," I offered.

Gloria stirred the onions again and rested the spatula on the counter before turning to face me. "He certainly has room. I'm sure you can stay as long as you need. This is a tough time to find a rental."

"I'll say. It's my own fault. I got annoyed with my last landlord for trying to raise the rent too high. I should've been a little more strategic about that argument," I said with a roll of my eyes.

Gloria grinned and shrugged. "I think some of the landlords around here do that just to snag the tourist money when they can. Levi mentioned you own Kick A** Construction with Amelia Masters. Is that right?"

"Sure is," I said, a sense of pride welling inside. I loved my job, and I loved working with Amelia.

"You two run one of the best construction companies in town. I told Brad he needs to hire you for the new garage he wants to build. Mind if I ask him to check with you about that?"

"Anytime. Just let us know when. We're filled up for this year, but it's getting late to start any new projects as it is. We could schedule it for next spring."

"I'll have him chat with you when he comes in. He likes to take care of everything himself, but a big project like that is too much as far as I'm concerned. Back to you though, looking for rentals now is bad timing, but with summer winding down, it's a good time to look for property over the winter. Anyone who didn't manage to sell over the summer will be more willing to negotiate."

"I've thought about that. I'll have to figure out the best timing."

Gloria nodded and then glanced over her shoulder when the kitchen door opened. I hadn't noticed the steady sound of wood stacking and chopping from outside had ceased. Levi and his father stepped through the door. The moment my eyes landed on Levi, my low belly clenched. With his hair tousled and his cheeks ruddy from the cool, late summer evening air, looking at him set need to humming inside of me.

The crisp scent of spruce gusted into the kitchen as his father closed the door behind them. Levi carried a woodsy, musky odor with him. His scent was pure octane to the lust that burned inside of me whenever he was near.

Don't be silly Lucy. You can't be sitting here lusting after him in front of his parents.

My body's response was swift. *Sure I can. You can't talk me out of it.*

The battle between my mind and body was raging these days. I took another sip of wine, willing myself to ignore the need spinning through my veins.

Gloria stirred the onions again before looking back to Levi and his father. "Well boys, is all the wood stacked?"

Levi's father tossed his work gloves in a basket by the door and hung his jacket, kicking his boots off in unison with Levi. He stepped to Gloria's side and dropped a kiss in the curve of her neck, only then answering. "Of course it is."

"We moved all of it under the woodshed, and I also filled the rack out on the porch. You're ready for winter," Levi added.

Gloria grinned as Levi stepped past her to

open the refrigerator and pull out a beer. "Need one, Dad?" he called over his shoulder.

"Sure thing," Brad replied, slipping onto a stool beside the kitchen island.

Levi spun back to the refrigerator, handing his father a beer and then walking to the table to slide into a chair at an angle across from me. His eyes met mine as he arched a brow. I hoped he couldn't tell I was wrestling with my almost constant desire for him.

Ignoring the heat on my cheeks, I smiled. "How was it?"

How was it? He was stacking wood. How could it be? Oh shut up.

I scolded my inner critic to stop nit-picking everything I said.

"Safe to say between work earlier and this, I'll sleep well tonight," he said with a grin before glancing to his father. "Hey Dad, you should talk to Lucy about the garage."

His eyes flicked back to me. "Dad wants a garage, so I told him he should have you and Amelia take care of it for him. Maybe next spring."

Before I could reply, his father was joining us at the table. "Gloria won't let me build it myself. She says the project is too much," Brad explained with a wry grin. "Honestly, she's probably right. I'm not as young as I used to be. I'd love to set up a time to chat with you and Amelia about getting the project on your schedule for next year."

"Of course. Amelia usually handles the planning upfront. I'll have her give you a call. We can slot you in for next spring. Sound good?"

"Sure does," he offered.

Levi's eyes caught mine, the heat banked there hot enough to singe me from across the table. Restless and flushed, I stood abruptly and excused myself to go to the restroom. I splashed cold water on my face and held my wrists under the water—anything to cool me down.

I stared at my reflection in the mirror. My cheeks were flushed, and my hair had come loose from its ponytail, tendrils dangling around my face. After drying my hands, I smoothed my hair back and took a deep breath, fortifying myself to get through dinner with Levi's parents without looking like a foolish, lovesick girl. It didn't help matters at all to know, deep down in the parts of my heart I'd kept locked away, that I might just be that.

When I returned to the kitchen, Gloria was serving plates with caribou and sautéed onions and mushrooms in gravy over rice. It was absolutely delicious. I glanced over to her between bites.

"This is amazing," I offered.

Levi caught my eye and winked before glancing to his mother. "Lucy's not much of a cook."

"I already fessed up," I added with a grin. "I figured you invited me over tonight out of pity."

"Of course not. It was for the company, but I did know if I didn't you'd probably eat soup out of a can for dinner."

Gloria gasped. "Soup out of the can?" she asked, her tone disbelieving

I shrugged sheepishly. "My mother wasn't much of a cook, and I'm not either."

"How is your mother?" Gloria asked conversationally.

"I haven't seen her in a few weeks. I didn't..."

My words trailed off because I was slightly confused to have Gloria ask about my mother.

"She and I are in a knitting group together," Gloria added, as if guessing my train of thought.

That was news to me. Though my mother hadn't cooked much, the one domestic thing she did was knit. It sounded as if she'd expanded her social circle more than I'd known. I kept my expression controlled and polite. I didn't want the awkwardness of my not-so-close relationship with my mother to be obvious. I wondered if Gloria knew I was a largely absent daughter as pangs of guilt stabbed at me.

"I didn't know you knew her well," I offered, uncertain what else to share.

Gloria nodded and smiled as she took a sip of wine. "Well, I've only just gotten to know her this last year. Janet started that knitting group and badgered me into it. Really, I don't know why we say we knit. It's mostly an excuse to get together, but that's how I met your mother. She's so proud of you."

I was suddenly slammed with curiosity. I didn't dare to pelt Gloria with my questions, so I nodded politely and smiled, relieved when Levi's father began asking questions about my opinion on what he wanted to do with the garage.

Conversation carried on, the moment that was likely awkward solely for me passing. Dinner with Levi's parents was comfortable and relaxed. I was more relaxed than I ever could've imagined I'd be having dinner with any man's family.

I oddly liked it, and I shied away from thinking about that. After we finished and Gloria was swatting the rest of us away from helping her clean up, she commented to Levi, "I told Lucy I was sure you'd let her stay as long as she needed over the winter. I think she should find some property and build anyway. Anything else is wasting money around here."

A flash of heat raced through me. I couldn't believe she had volunteered Levi to let me stay at his place for the entire winter. I almost spit out the sip of wine I'd just taken. Levi's eyes flicked to mine, a subtle gleam in them.

"Of course she can. I told her she could stay as long as she needs. Why don't you just plan on it?" he asked conversationally.

Talk about awkward. There was no polite way for me to respond, especially not with the heat burning in Levi's gaze sending sparks flying through me.

"I'll play it by ear and see what happens," I managed with a polite smile, willing the flush away from my cheeks even though I knew it was futile.

What I didn't dare say was there was this

crazy little part of me—a crazy part that had suddenly gotten vocal—that was practically jumping up and down with joy. A whole winter staying at Levi's would be heaven, pure heaven. I'd pretty much given up trying to talk myself out of the idea that I could get him out of my system.

LEVI

Later that night, I rolled my truck to a stop, glancing in my rear view mirror as Lucy's headlights reflected in the driveway behind me. It wasn't quite dark yet. Dinner at my parents generally didn't run too late. I turned my engine off and climbed out, walking around to meet Lucy once her truck rolled to a stop beside mine.

Her cheeks were flushed, and her hair windblown. Before we left, my father had insisted on taking her on a walk through my mother's gardens. He liked to show them off because he knew how much my mother loved them. She grew everything that could be grown in this part of Alaska, from vegetables to apple and cherry trees to perennials scattered about the property.

Lucy looked up at me once she closed the truck door behind her. "That was nice. Thanks for inviting me," she said simply.

My body was an engine on high idle whenever she was near. I couldn't be around her and not want her. In fact, I'd had to will my cock into submission in front of my parents.

I was fully expecting a phone call from my mother tomorrow. Perceptive as she was, I didn't doubt for a minute she'd picked up on the vibration between Lucy and me.

My father had straight up asked me about Lucy, starting off with, "So you like her a lot, then?"

My dad wasn't one to mince words, or avoid a topic. I'd considered not saying anything, but it seemed silly when he knew me so well. So I'd fessed up and told him the plain truth—she was the first woman I'd ever met who made me think about what he'd said to me all those years ago—that I'd know when I met the right woman.

He'd smiled slowly, his eyes warm. "Not too hard to see why. She's a lovely girl. Tough one though."

When I asked him what he meant, he

simply said, "You're going to have to earn her."

I replayed his words as I looked at Lucy and considered that I was half in love with her already. She'd slipped into my heart, and I hadn't even been trying to defend it. It was that fast and that easy, and I knew it in my bones. I just needed to not screw it up.

———

We stared at each other in the wispy light of dusk. The sky was almost dark, faded pink streaks from the last of the sun's glory disappearing with the stars and the moon. I stepped to her, catching her hand in mine and reeling her to me.

I meant to say something, but I didn't. The moment she was close, she tensed briefly. She was wound so tightly most of the time, and I wanted her to know she could let her guard down with me. I brushed her hair back from her face and slid my hand down her spine, careful not to jostle her wrist.

She noticed, her eyes catching mine as her sky blue gaze darkened. "It doesn't hurt. You don't have to be careful."

There was a hint of a smile teasing her

lips, letting me know she wasn't annoyed. A damn miracle.

I lifted a shoulder in a slow shrug and dipped my head, my lips feathering across her cheek. I was simply unable to resist the urge to touch her.

"Maybe not, but there's nothing wrong with being careful." My next words slipped out unbidden. "Just let me take care of you."

A thrum of tension rippled through her body before she sighed softly. I dipped my head lower, dusting kisses along her neck. Her tension melted as she went soft against me, her good arm sliding around my waist.

I meant to take it slow. But then her tongue tangled sensuously with mine and her hand slid under my shirt to explore my chest. Her touch was like lightning, sending streaks of electricity shimmering on the surface of my skin everywhere she touched. Our kiss went wild. My hand tangled in her hair while I slid the other down her spine to cup her lush bottom, pulling her tight against my arousal.

Lucy drove me insane. I was hanging onto a thin thread of control. After hours of trying to contain my desire, need was lashing at me.

I lifted her against me. Her legs curled easily around my hips as she wrapped her arms around my neck. Her gasps and breathy moans spurred me on. Hell if I knew how, but I managed to walk with her kissing me. I needed her more than air. Our kiss was a hot, wet tangle.

Thank fuck she was lightweight. I managed to get up the stairs and through the door without sending us both tumbling to the ground. Kicking the door shut behind me, I spun around. For a beat, I worried I was too rough when I heard the door rattle as her back slammed against it. I started to pause and draw away.

"Oh God, don't go gentle on me," she muttered, her voice husky.

Another deep, electrifying kiss and then she was shimmying down from my hold and tearing my jeans open. Before I could scramble to take control, she shoved my briefs down and spun around, pushing me against the door.

Her hand curled around my cock as it sprang free. I groaned, my cock rock hard with need, pre-cum dripping and running down the tip. I looked down at her, her hair a wild tangle around her face, her cheeks flushed and her lips swollen.

Her tongue darted out as she drew it in a swirl around the tip of my cock, swiping up the drop of cum, a sly smile claiming her lips. My knees almost buckled. I brushed her hair back from her face, barely hanging on to my control as she drew me into her mouth.

With the warm, wet suction of her mouth drawing me in and out, her hand curling around the base of my cock, and her wet grip sliding in rhythm with her mouth, she pushed me close to my breaking point. I thundered toward my release faster than I wanted.

"Lucy, I need..."

Whatever I meant to say was lost in the wave of pleasure crashing over me as I came in her mouth. She drank in my release, drawing back as I sagged against the door.

Her tongue swiped across her lips, sending another lash of need through me. I didn't think I would ever get enough of her. I drew her up, lifting her against me. I meant to take her upstairs, to make love to her properly. But she was having none of that.

She tugged at my shirt, almost knocking me off balance. Easing her down beside the couch with a laugh, I yanked off her clothing, tearing her blouse open and shoving her jeans down over her hips. I was still surprised every time I saw her underwear—tonight they were bright pink cotton.

I reached between her thighs to find the

cotton soaked and sticky with her arousal. I dragged my fingers across the fabric, savoring the hiss of her breath. Biting her lip with a grin, she glanced to me. I stared at her as she stood before me, her shirt hanging open, her nipples taut against the silk of her bra. Leaning forward, I laved my tongue across the silk and over the tight little bead. She cried out, arching into me, and I couldn't wait. I needed her bare. Flinging her bra off and shoving her panties down, I spun her around where we stood. Kicking the pink cotton loose from her ankle, her hands curled over the back of the sofa.

With need roaring through me, the sweet arch of her spine and the sight of her lush ass nearly did me in.

Chapter Twenty-Four

LUCY

My hands gripped the back of the couch, my fingers digging into the cushioned fabric. Levi untangled his fingers from my hair, his palm sliding down my spine in a path of burning heat. I arched under his touch, frantic for more.

The hot, velvety skin of his shaft brushed against my bottom before he slid his hand between my thighs, nudging my legs apart with his knee as his fingers delved into my folds. I was soaked with need for him.

I barely recognized myself as I cried out, moaning his name. Suddenly, Levi muttered something else before stepping back swiftly. I started to straighten, glancing over my shoulder. "Where..."

"Condom," he bit it out gruffly. "I just have to run upstairs."

I shook my head sharply. "No need. I'm on the pill."

He stared at me, his eyes boring into mine. I suddenly felt vulnerable.

"I don't know what I was thinking. I mean..." I started to say.

He shook his head sharply, his hands curling around my hips again.

I'd been on the pill for years. It was more a convenience thing than anything. Despite that, I'd never had sex without a condom. Not even the fateful time I lost my virginity. Although the guy had been a jerk about it after the fact, he had used a condom.

I stared at Levi over my shoulder. His hand on my hip was a hot brand, searing us together. I didn't want him to run upstairs and grab a condom. I didn't want anything that would make me stop and think. I shook my head again, nudging my hips back against him.

"I need you," I said roughly.

I broke free from his gaze. It was too intense, the moment too intimate.

"Okay," he said softly. "Are you..."

I cut him off, anticipating he was about to

ask if I was okay with this. "I wouldn't have said anything if I wasn't."

I didn't want to think, I wanted to lose myself in sensation. He stepped closer, the head of his cock sliding through my folds. He was hard and thick, despite having come in my mouth only moments ago. I felt a wash of relief, knowing perhaps he was as needy for me as I was for him. He teased me, coating his cock with my juices as he dragged it back and forth.

On another low moan, pleading for him to give me what I needed, he finally did. He sank inside, slow and sure, stretching and filling me. Seating himself deeply, he held still for a beat, his hands cupping my hips. I arched back, pressing against him. His palm slid up my spine, his touch a blaze of heat, sending sparks flying into the fire already burning inside.

I was aflame inside and out, spiraling out of control, and I didn't care. My need for him was like a storm inside, pushing me into a frenzy. His hand laced into my hair as he started to stroke into me, drawing out fully and sinking in again and again. The pull and slide inside my channel had me dancing on the edge. He murmured hot, dirty words.

"Lucy, you make me crazy. You're so fucking hot."

When I groaned on the heels of a rough drive into me, he muttered, "Your pussy feels so fucking good, so tight."

All the while, I gasped, moaned and cried his name with every thrust. This wasn't a gentle claiming, it was rough and hard—exactly what I needed. This was the only way to slake my endless need for him.

On the heels of a deep surge, I felt him start to tighten. He eased his grip on my hip, reaching his hand around and swirling his fingers over my clit.

My climax crashed over me, the pleasure hitting me like sparks on metal, scattering through me everywhere. I was nearly limp from it, barely hearing his guttural cry as the heat of his release filled me.

I stood there, my hands gripping the back of the couch with my head bowed as I caught my breath. Levi slowly straightened, his hands holding me steady at the hips. My heart drummed out a wild beat, and it wasn't simply from the exertion. I suddenly wanted to cry, not from sadness, but from the depth of emotion coursing through me.

I didn't know what to do with any of it. So I simply tried to catch my breath, having no sense of how much time was passing. I didn't realize I was getting cold until he spoke.

"You're cold," Levi said, his hands sliding over my skin, his touch warm and comforting. I lifted my head, glancing over my shoulder and hoping the dim lighting masked the tears pressing at the backs of my eyes.

"I guess so."

He drew back, yet before I had a chance to miss the feel of him filling me, he was lifting me in his arms and carrying me upstairs. He almost stumbled on the stairs.

I giggled, feeling emotional and giddy. "That's what you get for trying to walk up the stairs with your jeans halfway on."

I felt his smile against my hair. "So true," he said as he cleared the top step and quickly walked into the bathroom.

Within a few seconds, steam was filling the bathroom, and he was tugging me into the shower after pausing to help me remove my brace. Hot water pounded down over us. It was a few moments before I absorbed the fact that this was now the second time I'd showered with him. I'd never showered with anyone else before.

Me, the queen of one night stands, once a year at best. If that. I'd never let myself share the intimacy of a shower. I looked over as he leaned his head under the water to rinse the shampoo out, water and soap bubbles running down over his body.

It shouldn't even be legal for him to look the way he did. My mouth went dry just looking at him now, and it had only been moments since my channel had been quaking around his cock. I should be satiated, but then I was starting to doubt I ever could be when it came to Levi.

His skin was bronzed, his body hardened, yet not in the polished way of a man who worked out. Rather, his fitness was pure, raw masculinity. He worked a dangerous job, a job that demanded rugged strength and toughness. With his eyes closed as the water poured over him, I looked my fill, my greedy eyes coasting over his muscled chest, down along his hips to his strong legs. Even in rest, there wasn't an inch of him that wasn't hard. A grin curled the corner of my mouth when I corrected myself. At this particular moment, his cock wasn't hard...although it usually was around me.

I'd never thought much about the power I could have over a man. Yet, with Levi, I felt powerful and vulnerable at once.

His eyes opened as he lifted his head,

catching my gaze through the water and steam. In a flash, his hand curled around mine, and he reeled me up against him, dipping his head and catching my lips in a kiss. My heart thudded hard in my chest. I couldn't control any of this, and I didn't know how.

I scrambled for purchase inside and then stopped bothering. I let myself tumble into the feel of his hard muscled body against mine, the hot water and steam cocooning us in our own little world. I could kiss him for days and days and days.

When he drew back, brushing my wet, tangled hair back off my forehead, I caught his eyes. "You're really good at that."

He grinned, one of those delectable, belly flipping grins of his. "Good at what?"

"Kissing."

"I don't think it's me. I think it's us."

The moment felt suddenly heavy. I wanted to scoot away, yet I couldn't. Because no matter how much that scared me, the need to be close to him overrode every other instinct. With his eyes locked on mine, without a word spoken, it was as if he sensed the anxiety starting to bloom inside of me.

With a slight smile, he lightened the moment. "Well, you're warm now."

I was not a giggler, but Levi made me giggle. A lot more than I wanted to admit. With a giggle, I looked up at him through the steam. "I am."

He turned the water off, stepped out and handed me the towel.

By some miracle, he'd remembered to remind me to remove my brace before we showered. I didn't want to sleep with it on and said as much. He opened his mouth as if to argue and then snapped it shut.

"Since you didn't tell me what to do, I'll wear it. I can't wait to see the doctor next week."

Next thing I knew, he was bundling us into bed. His bed was soft, the cotton sheets cool against my skin. I didn't even bother not to burrow against him. Sleeping with him was like having my own personal heater. I was trying to settle in without my brace bumping him when his voice came above my head.

"I don't even notice it. Once I'm in bed, all I do is sleep when I'm with you. Well except for sex," he offered.

I could feel his smile against my hair. I giggled and let my hand fall against his chest. I fell asleep easily, feeling warm and protected in his embrace.

Chapter Twenty-Five

LEVI

A few days later, I rapped quickly on the kitchen door to my parents' house before stepping inside. "Hey Mom," I called. "Got your text."

The sound of footsteps reached me as she came down the stairs and crossed the hallway into the kitchen. Her blonde hair was pulled back in a bun with a pencil.

"Hi hon," she said as she stepped to my side and pecked me on the cheek. "Coffee?"

"Of course," I replied as I shrugged out of my jacket and tossed it on the coat rack by the door. "So what's wrong with your dishwasher?"

"Well, if I knew what was wrong with it, I wouldn't have called you."

I chuckled. "So true. You like to fix things yourself when you can, just like Lucy."

I hadn't meant for that to slip out. Oh well.

My mother turned away from the coffee pot, handing me a mug. Straight black coffee, just how I liked it. I took a swallow and prepared myself for her to comment on what I'd just said.

She didn't disappoint. "Lucy seems like an independent woman. I like her," she said pointedly.

Her perceptive gaze assessed me, but I didn't have anything to hide.

"I'm glad you like her," I finally said. "I do too."

She smiled slowly. "I noticed."

I set my coffee down and stepped to the dishwasher. After fiddling with it for a moment, I glanced to her. "Did you check the drain?"

"I tried, but I can't get it unscrewed."

Opening the door, I knelt down and leaned inside the dishwasher. I heard her leaning against the counter nearby while I worked. The drain was the likely culprit, and it wasn't coming loose easily.

"In all seriousness, Lucy is wonderful. I asked her mother about her," she offered.

I groaned, wishing my mother wasn't so damn curious. With my head inside the dishwasher at this point, she couldn't see me roll my eyes, which was probably a good thing.

"Mom, I know you care about me, and I know you're going to be nosy, but don't make Lucy uncomfortable. Please," I said, my voice muffled by the dishwasher.

"Jody won't say anything. I've gotten to know her pretty well. After you brought Lucy over for dinner, I just wanted to know a little bit more about her. She's lovely and bright, but she certainly keeps to herself. She seemed a little, well I don't know, guarded? I wouldn't quite say she was shy, but..."

I leaned out of the dishwasher with a handful of gunk that had been crammed in the drain. My mother set her coffee down and quickly grabbed the trashcan for me. I stood and washed my hands in the sink.

"Guarded might be the way to put it. What were you hoping her mom was going to tell you?" I asked.

I couldn't help it, but I was curious as hell. Lucy may not talk about it much, but it was clear she wasn't particularly close to her mother.

While my mother cleaned up, I checked the dishwasher again. After resetting the control panel, it started right up. I grabbed my coffee and leaned against the counter, waiting for my mother.

Tossing a paper towel in the trash, she returned to her spot by the counter and took a healthy swallow of coffee. "Well, I didn't know what her mother would tell me, but I learned a lot. They moved up here after Lucy was in foster care for a year."

My mouth dropped open as I stared at her. "What?" I finally managed.

"You look as shocked as I was. Her father was abusive, and her mother didn't leave him for years. According to her mother, he was only violent to Lucy once, but that's what landed her in foster care."

Anger sliced through me, hot and searing. My fingers gripped the edge of the counter tightly, the physical need to punch something coursing through me. Yet, the man I needed to punch was nowhere near, and it would definitely *not* be okay if I punched the wall in my mother's kitchen.

I was reeling inside, trying to wrap my brain around too much at once. My mother's eyes caught mine. I must've looked blank because I was practically numb, so she continued. "Her mother didn't have the strength to leave her father, so Lucy went to foster care for a year. They moved to Willow Brook when Jody finally got the nerve to leave. She said she knew she needed to leave the state to get away, so that's what they did."

I gulped the rest of my coffee, needing the bitterness. I was knocked sideways inside, scrambling for purchase. Restless, I pushed off the counter and helped myself to another cup of coffee.

"Her mother knows you brought Lucy over for dinner because I mentioned it. She was thrilled to hear Lucy's seeing you."

Here my mother paused, long enough to cue me to the fact she likely knew more and wasn't telling me. "What the hell aren't you telling me?"

She eyed me carefully, setting her coffee down. "You need to hear it from Lucy, not me."

I stared at my mother. "Bullshit."

Her gaze softened. "Hon, her mother told me in confidence, mostly because I think she worries about Lucy."

Her gaze was calm, steady and implacable. I took a swift gulp of coffee, trying like hell to absorb all of this and feeling helpless.

"I'm guessing it would be crazy if I flew to California to kick her dad's ass?"

My mother's eyes were sad as she looked

at me. "It wouldn't be crazy, but I don't think it would help. Unless Lucy cared for you to stir things up like that, it wouldn't change anything," she said softly.

"I could beat him the way he beat her," I said my voice low, the anger vibrating through me.

My mother stepped to me, cupping my face in her hands as she looked up at me. "I love you. You were a good little boy, and you're a good man. I completely understand why you might want to do that, but you need to let this be. Unless Lucy wants you to do that, just stay out of it," she said, her hands sliding down to squeeze my shoulders before she stepped back.

Emotion and anger wound together in a fierce storm inside of me. Yet, I knew my mother was right. This was Lucy's history, and I couldn't storm into it like that. She moved here when she was a senior in high school, so it was over ten years ago now.

"How do I talk to Lucy about this?" I asked, looking to my mother.

My mother sipped her coffee, her gaze considering. "There's a time and a place for everything, and you'll know the time."

I took another gulp of coffee, savoring

the bitterness, just what I needed in this moment. I knew she was right. I would have to wait, and hopefully Lucy would tell me herself.

Chapter Twenty-Six

LEVI

The following week, I walked up the porch steps, gratified to discover Lucy had arrived home before me. I had learned today my crew was scheduled for a rotation on a fire up in the Alaskan Interior that just wouldn't quit. The winds had shifted again, sending the fire back in the direction of a cluster of Alaskan Native villages.

I wanted more time with Lucy before I left for what would probably be more than a week. Closing the door behind me, I looked over to see her standing at the kitchen counter with groceries scattered across it. She looked confused. My eyes flicked down to notice the distinctive blue brace was gone from her wrist. Kicking off my boots and hanging my jacket on a hook by the door, I walked straight to her, dipping my head and dropping a kiss along the side of her neck.

I couldn't say why, but the last few days, she'd seemed easier around me, as if she was finally letting down her guard.

"Your brace is gone," I murmured as I slipped my arms around her, my hands resting on the soft curve of her belly.

Her eyes canted up to mine from the side. "Finally," she said, a slight smile gracing her lips.

"Anything you need to worry about with it?" I asked

One of her shoulders shrugged against my chest. "Just to take it easy and not overdo it."

"Ah, I'm sure you can handle that," I replied with a chuckle.

She swatted at my chest with the back of her hand. "I definitely can!"

I scanned the collection of groceries on the counter. She hadn't gone grocery shopping since my last observation about her interesting choice of groceries.

"What's all this for?" I asked.

"I'm making dinner," she announced firmly.

"Oh," I said, trying to keep my concern out of my tone.

I glanced from the groceries to her, a smile tugging at the corners of my mouth. Her gaze flicked up to mine, and she snagged her bottom lip with her teeth, her eyes glinting with humor.

I eyed what was scattered about on the counter, a collection of vegetables and some rice. "What are you making?" I finally asked.

"Chicken fajitas." There was a long pause before she spoke again. "But I forgot the chicken," she explained, a sheepish grin claiming her lips.

"Can't really make chicken fajitas without the chicken," I observed.

She shook her head with a sigh. "I don't suppose I can."

She turned in my arms. "I wanted to surprise you. Your mom told me you love chicken fajitas."

When her eyes met mine with a flush blooming on her cheeks, my heart squeezed —hard—in my chest.

I was screwed. I'd fallen so in love with Lucy, it was all I could do not to blurt it out right now. But I had to be careful with her. She was skittish by nature. It meant so much that somehow she found out this was one of my favorite childhood meals and wanted to make it for me.

I tried to imagine the conversation with my mother. That Lucy somehow discovered this small detail sent emotion spinning around my heart and knotting in my throat. I swallowed past it.

"I have some chicken in the freezer," I offered, striving to keep my tone casual. "Have you ever made chicken fajitas before?"

She shook her head quickly and then reached into the front pocket of her jeans, pulling out of scrap of paper and handing it to me.

Scribbled in her writing was my mom's recipe. I knew it by heart because my mother made it so many times when I was a kid and still did.

"How did you get this recipe?"

When I looked back over at Lucy, her cheeks were still flushed. "I asked your mom. I wanted to surprise you but you got home earlier than I thought. I also don't know how to cook very well, but you know that."

"I'll help," I offered.

The smile that claimed her lips was so wide, I didn't bother trying not to pull her close. She giggled as I lifted her against me and stole her smile with my kiss.

———

Later that night, after what would go down as one of the best nights ever, I lay in bed with Lucy against my chest. Her skin was damp against mine, and our breath was heaving. My cock still buried deep inside her slick channel. I'd just spent myself inside of her while she flew apart in my arms. Her legs were curled against my sides, and her lush curves pressed against me where she collapsed after crying out my name.

As the thundering of my heartbeat slowed and I managed to catch my breath, I heard Ham scurrying into the bedroom, his little feet scratching on the hardwood flooring. I felt Lucy smile against my chest.

"I love that you have a hamster," she said with a little laugh, her breath gusting against my skin.

Running a hand through her hair and down her spine in a slow pass, a smile tugged at the corners of my mouth.

"Jasmine gave him to me. I thought it was silly, but she said I needed company. My sister's kinda bossy sometimes. I'm glad though. He's a fun little guy."

I paused, realizing I needed to tell her I would be leaving for the backcountry in a few days. I didn't want to go. She must've felt me tense because she lifted her head, resting her chin on my chest.

The moonlight was cast through my window, so I could see her eyes clearly, blue in the silvery light.

"What?" she asked.

"I was about to say the only challenge is having someone stop by and take care of Ham when I'm gone for work. Usually my parents do it, but it reminded me we're heading out the day after tomorrow to deal with a fire up north."

"Tomorrow?" she asked, her eyes widening slightly.

I could feel her heartbeat kick up a notch against my chest.

"Not tomorrow. The day after." I paused, considering my words. I kicked my caution to the curb. "I was hoping I could ask you to take care of Ham while I'm gone."

She held still, but I could feel the tension vibrating in her body and could practically see the wheels turning in her head. She thought so hard about everything.

After a beat, when I was starting to get nervous she was going to tell me she couldn't, she nodded.

"Of course. I'm here anyway," she said softly, her eyes slightly guarded.

"Thank you. Ham likes you."

Lucy giggled, that guarded look in her eyes dissipating. "You think?"

"Sure he does. He napped on your lap earlier."

After dinner, we'd lounged on the sofa for a little bit, and Ham had, in fact, snuggled up on her lap.

My hand was still sliding up and down her back in slow passes. She watched me, her eyes coasting over my face.

"I'm sure I can find my own place soon," she suddenly said.

For a flash, my heart stuttered and a sharp ache pierced me. My hand stilled and then I forced it to keep stroking over her silky skin. I wanted to say, *"Don't leave. Stay with me."*

Yet, I didn't. "You're welcome to stay here through the winter if you need," I heard myself saying.

Her gaze scanned my face as words and emotion knotted in my throat. For a moment, I thought she wasn't going to reply, but then she nodded.

"Thank you," she said softly. "I'm still looking for a rental. Frankly, I might have better luck finding a seasonal rental for the winter."

I swallowed against the emotion tightening every muscle in my body and forced myself to keep my touch light and easy. I wanted to hold her tight and tell her she didn't have to do everything alone.

She looked at me, chewing the inside of her cheek, a habit I'd noticed she had when she was worrying about something.

Her fingers traced lightly across my chest. "So you leave the day after tomorrow?" At my nod, she continued. "For how long?"

"We don't always know. Usually it's a week or two, but we may stay longer depending on what's happening with the fire and the weather conditions."

In the quiet, she startled me when she lifted a fingertip and traced my brows. "Oh, well, I hope you're not gone too long."

Her words hit me hard, and I wanted to say more, but the uncertainty in her eyes held me back. I simply nodded.

Her touch slid down along my cheekbone, coming to stop in the curve of my neck. She rested her head against my chest again, her breath feathering against my skin. We fell asleep like that.

Chapter Twenty-Seven

LUCY

The following day, I should've been in a good mood. I was finally cleared to do more than light duty. I'd gotten nothing more than a mild scolding from my doctor to take it easy and not push too hard.

A cool summer breeze gusted across my face as I worked. I loved working in construction because it meant being outside. The physical exertion was also satisfying and tended to nudge me out of my tendency to worry. The physicality of the work and the calm predictability suited me. There was nothing uncertain about measuring a two-by-four for a cut. Everything was laid out in neat, organized plans.

If only life could be like that, then maybe

I could relax. I'd once seen a therapist, back when I was in foster care. She'd been nice enough, but at the time I'd been so bitter and just tired of life. No child should be so tired by the time they're in high school that all they hoped for was a boring life. Even though I'd finally escaped my father, I had to worry about my mother, which I did all the time. I was always on edge, waiting for the next shoe to drop in foster care.

My therapist had talked to me about trauma and how it could make you hyper-vigilant. She'd described that as always being on the alert for everything around me, and she'd thought that was what I had going on. Even though I hated, absolutely hated, admitting I had any weaknesses, she'd zeroed in on precisely how I felt all the time. I couldn't recall a single time in my life when I could relax and not worry about what might come next.

Anxiety bloomed in my chest. You see, things felt so good with Levi. Even though I'd been guarding against it, I'd let myself relax and enjoy it a little too much.

His pending departure, entirely expected given his line of work, had me on edge, worried and scrambling for purchase inside emotionally.

This is why you can't have nice things.

My snide, ever-knowing, doubtful voice taunted me.

I was saved from my internal battles when Amelia paused by my side. "I think we have enough now," she said a hint of laughter in her voice.

I glanced up to find her amber eyes crinkling at the corners with her smile. Looking down, I realized I'd cut more two-by-four's than we needed for this particular room. Turning back to her, I rolled my eyes with a laugh.

"I lost track. It felt so good to have two hands."

She didn't say anything, her gaze assessing my face. I inwardly groaned. Amelia knew me better than anyone else.

"You okay?"

The moment she asked, emotion slammed into my chest. I was terrified. I'd let myself fall in love with Levi, and I hadn't even noticed it was happening. I should've known better, but then I'd never been in love, never even considered it might happen to me.

For a beat, I contemplated dismissing her question. But, she would know.

I finished the cut on the two-by-four in hand and leaned it against the wall along with the rest of the tidy rows of stacked lumber. Turning, I rested my hips against the table saw stand and looked up at her, crossing my arms.

"I'm in over my head," I said with a sigh.

Simply saying it aloud set my heart to thudding against my ribs.

Amelia leaned on a sawhorse across from me, quickly pulling the elastic out of her ponytail and smoothing her hair back from her face where it had fallen loose. As she tied it up again, she eyed me.

"Are we talking about Levi?" she finally asked.

I nodded as hot tears pricked at the backs of my eyes.

"Is that a bad thing?"

I nodded, perhaps frantically. Her gaze softened as she stared at me. "Why is that bad? Levi's a good guy. Cade's also pretty convinced he's in love with you."

My heart started beating so hard and fast it hurt. Hope flew like birds from a cage inside of me—the cage where I'd locked hope away many years ago.

"Why would Cade think that?" I asked, my voice thick with emotion.

When I spoke, I didn't realize tears had

started to roll down my cheeks until Amelia stepped to me and pulled me into a hug.

When she drew back, she took a deep breath and sighed. "Well then, I guess I'm right too."

"About what?" I asked, dragging a sleeve across my cheeks.

"Oh, I kinda thought if you ever let yourself give Levi a chance, you'd fall for him. Before you even worry about it, I didn't say anything to Cade. It's more than just sex, although I bet the sex is good," she said with a grin as she stepped back, resting her hips against the sawhorse again.

I swallowed against the emotion bundling tightly in my chest and throat. "I think maybe I am. I can't do this though."

"Why not? I got over myself with Cade. You can too," she said softly.

I shook my head and tried to catch my breath. My heart felt as if it had been scraped raw, the pain stinging.

"It's better when it's just me," I finally said.

Amelia leaned her head back up to stare at the sky as an eagle called and flew above us, its wings casting a wide shadow on the ground below. I took several deep breaths, but the pain in my heart wasn't easing.

When her eyes leveled with mine again, I spoke. "He said the crew's been called out after today, probably for two weeks."

"I know. Cade's crew is leaving with them. Now you know how I feel. It sucks," she said bluntly. "I try to tell myself that they know better than probably anybody else how to take care of themselves and how to get out of a jam. But it doesn't make it any easier."

Tightening my arms, I nodded. "Levi said I could stay for the winter."

"How is that a problem? You need somewhere to stay. I mean, you're always welcome at our place once we have our boiler installed, but he's definitely got more space than we do."

"I can't," I replied, shaking my head sharply.

"It's okay to need someone," Amelia finally said.

The word *need* lashed at me. I instinctively wanted to punch back at it. I hated needing anyone. It represented everything that went wrong for my mother. She couldn't scrabble together the courage to leave my father because she thought she needed him, that she didn't have what it took to be a single mother. I couldn't see past the reality that my father had worn her sense of self down to nothing. I couldn't believe there could be a healthy sense of need.

"This is too much for me to talk about it," I said abruptly.

Spinning away, I needlessly straightened the rows of two-by-four's leaning against the wall.

"Can we change the subject?" I asked without looking at Amelia.

"Of course," she finally said. "You know I'm here when you want to talk."

I almost laughed. She didn't say *if,* she said *when.* That was the kind of friend she was.

———

That night, I lay in bed beside Levi. Again. I'd given up any pretense of sleeping in the guestroom. Tonight, he'd taken me on the kitchen counter after we ate the leftovers from the chicken fajitas that he mostly cooked last night. All I'd really done was chop vegetables.

I was warm, relaxed and sated. His fingers were sifting through my hair where my head was tucked into his shoulder.

His voice nudged me out of my sleepy, mellow state. "Lucy?"

I lifted my head and glanced up. "Uh huh?" I asked.

"I'll miss you," he said gruffly, his eyes catching mine in the moonlight falling through the window.

For a moment, I was confused. My body still reverberating from the echoes of my climax, I'd conveniently forgotten he was leaving tomorrow. For at least two weeks. The time stretched before me in my mind, a chasm of distance between us.

The air felt heavy. I knew I was going to miss him – acutely.

But I wasn't ready for any of this, much less ready to talk to him about it. The look in his eyes was intent and searching. I felt as if he could see right into my heart—to the flawed, confused woman who didn't believe she deserved to have love in her life.

A pang of guilt stabbed at me. He had the courage to speak his feelings. He was a straightforward, direct person. Meeting his family had made things worse for me. Watching him with his parents had only reinforced what I already knew. I could see past his tendency to tease and see the core of him —a strong man with a good heart. He deserved to be with somebody who had more courage than I did.

After a moment, awareness flickered in his gaze. Without a word passing between us, it was as if he knew I was afraid. He wasn't going to push.

"I just thought you should know," he finally said.

I swallowed against the tightness in my chest, the pain pounding in my heart. I surprised myself.

"I'll miss you too."

His eyes widened slightly, and then he brushed my hair away from my face and lifted his head slightly, just enough to catch my lips with his.

The point of contact was soft, yet electrifying. My heart was pounding so hard, it felt as if I had just run a marathon.

He drew away, his head falling back against the pillows as his fingers slipped through my hair and down along my back. In a very short time, I'd become spoiled by his tendency to stroke my back as I fell asleep. His touch lulled me straight to sleep.

Sleep had never come easily to me, but with Levi, it did. My mind didn't run on a hamster wheel of anxiety and worry. Perhaps it was the physical closeness, the sensual satiation. It surprised me, if only because I knew I should be worrying—worrying about how comfortable I was, how I savored the feeling of being tangled up with him.

I shook my thoughts away, relaxing into the feel of his warm touch. My heartbeat slowed, and I tumbled into sleep.

Chapter Twenty-Eight

LUCY

Since Levi had left a few days ago, he'd called early on before they flew out of Fairbanks and when they were at their base camp. Like a lovesick idiot, I answered the phone. Every time. The first two calls, I'd managed to be normal. You know, I told him how my day went and that I fed Ham carrots. But then, there was the last call.

Just thinking about it, my face got hot. I'd replayed it a few hundred times and still couldn't get over it. I'd said something colossally stupid.

It all started when he told me he missed me. For a second, I let myself soak in his words. Then, it was like a boomerang inside. I couldn't let myself savor any of it. I missed him so much, my heart literally ached, and I was furious for it. I'd let down my guard, and now I'd set myself up. Because there was no way this could work. I didn't have it in me to do a relationship. The very idea terrified me.

When I didn't say anything, he pushed a little too much.

"Lucy, you know it wouldn't be so bad to actually talk about the fact there's something between us."

My simmering anger flashed hot. I hated talking about my feelings. And this? He wanted me to talk about us? No. Just no.

I supposed that was a normal thing for a person who was doing what we were doing to say. But I couldn't deal. At all.

Cue the stupid.

"You don't understand," I blurted out. "It's not okay. There is no happily ever after. Not in my world."

I heard his breath hiss. "Why would you say that?" he asked, sounding deflated.

Cornered and vulnerable, I lashed out because it was all I knew how to do.

"Levi, you have no fucking clue. You have the perfect family. Your parents are nice, and they're still together. They love you, and they would do anything for you. I'm happy for you. I really am. But that's not my family. My father was awful. He was verbally and emotionally abusive to my mother for my whole childhood. Sometimes he beat her up, and then he beat me up..."

I paused to catch my breath because all kinds of emotions I'd stuffed deep down were barreling though me so fast, I could hardly breathe. I didn't know if Levi actually asked why, but in my mind, he did. So I continued, my words pouring out like a runaway train.

"See, I was shy in high school. It was a big high school, and I didn't have many friends because we moved all the time. Like an idiot, I had a crush on a guy. He took me to a dance. I was on cloud nine, and I lost my virginity. That wasn't a bad thing, but then he told the whole school, and I got slut shamed like you wouldn't believe. I still don't know how, but somehow my fucking father found out. He'd hated my mother forever because she got pregnant in high school, and he blamed his whole shitty life on her for that. He was furious at me and said I was trying to do the same thing. I went to bed with two black eyes. Then, I went to foster care and that was the best thing that ever happened to me. That's what a mess my family was. The next best thing was when my mom finally got the nerve to leave my dad, and we moved to Willow Brook."

As soon as I stopped talking, there was a rushing sound in my ears. I wanted to scream and cry. I couldn't believe I'd just told him that. I didn't tell anyone this. Even Amelia only had bits and pieces.

Because he was a good man, Levi tried to be nice.

"Lucy, I'm sorry. That's terrible," he said, his voice careful as if he wasn't sure what to say.

Tears rolled hot down my cheeks. I had to get off the phone. "I have to go."

"No! Lucy, don't just hang up. Let me..."

I cut him off. "Let you what? Tell me it'll be okay? Let you feel bad for me? No! It's the past. It's over. But you have to understand not everyone gets the kind of life you had growing up. It's not all sunshine and roses."

"You're not even giving me a chance. I'm not gonna tell you what happened was okay. It wasn't. I can be sad something happened to you without feeling bad for you. Let me be there for you. Let..." He paused as he took a ragged breath. "Lucy, just let me love..."

I couldn't listen. It hurt too much. I hung up and wisely turned my phone off right away.

That had been a complete disaster. I was mortified. Letting out the worst part of my buried past made me feel more vulnerable when I already felt like I was skidding sideways inside when it came to him. The only upside was it reinforced what I needed to do. As soon as Levi came back, I had to move out.

LEVI

The sound of the helicopter blades whacking through the air had me glancing pointlessly toward the sky. Though I knew there was a helicopter flying above, I couldn't see a damn thing. The smoke was thick in the sky where we were, the wind gusting the smoke from the fire only a few miles away.

My crew was here with Cade's. This fire had ballooned out of control with the wind whipping it wildly. The interior of Alaska was mostly hundreds of miles of wilderness. Nothing but trees, better known as fuel when you're a hotshot firefighter.

It had been a full week since we'd flown up here, and I was exhausted, along with my entire crew. I heard my name and turned back to see Jesse approaching. It was hard to know what time of day it was. Even though it was late summer, in northern Alaska that still meant long days. Through the smoke above us, the sun was nothing but a hazy halo.

I took my gloves off and glanced at my watch to see that it was going on seven in the evening. Jesse reached my side, tugging his gear off of his face. With the smoke mostly blowing above our heads, it was safe to remove our respirators.

He nudged his chin beyond my shoulder. "That should be Fred coming down over there," he commented.

Fred Banks was a well-known bush pilot. He flew planes and helicopters and spent most of the summer working for hotshot firefighter crews all across Alaska. Flying might not be as physically taxing as what we did, but it was just as dangerous in the backcountry. Conditions could shift rapidly, and it was isolated out here.

We'd spent the last three days setting up firebreaks along two intersecting rivers in this area. Fred was due to pick us up and return us to a base camp where there was a gear tent, along with a medical tent and a place to sleep outside of the smoke for a few nights. If the weather held, we might be finishing up our rotation out here in the next few days.

I caught Jesse's eyes and clapped him on the shoulder. "Good. Let's head that way. You rounded up the rest of the guys?" I asked.

Jesse nodded and started walking, throwing his heavy bag of gear over his shoulder. He was one of my foremen, and I relied on him out in the field. Grabbing the chainsaw I'd been using, I slung my gear over my shoulders and walked at his side.

Lucy sashayed into my thoughts, as she did almost any free moment. I was thankful hard work kept me focused and distracted. Because otherwise I missed her so damn much, it hurt.

Missing her was akin to a physical ache, something I'd never experienced before. My mind spun back to our last night together. She'd startled me by saying she would miss me. The following morning, she'd become distant.

She'd been tense, and I'd wanted to wrap her in my arms, hold her tight and tell her not to worry. Yet, I knew she was worrying—about us, about me—and that I needed not to push too hard. I loved her independence, her strength, her intelligence and her willpower. It hurt me to recognize how she was terrified to allow herself to need anyone.

I'd been turning thoughts of her in my mind like a worry stone—contemplating how to get through the last of her reservations, how to get her to understand I didn't want to take anything from her. I simply wanted to be there for her, to love her.

I'd yet to come up with an answer on how to make any of that happen. Even now, I gave myself a mental shake. Not a damn thing I could do out here in the middle of the wilderness, facing down a fire.

I loved her. I sensed she loved me.

Yet, I knew that wasn't something she wanted to feel. My last call with her had been a disaster when we'd been at the base camp. There was no reception to speak of in the middle of the wilderness, but the base camp was within range of the cell towers in Fairbanks.

She'd gotten angry when I said I missed her and ended up blurting out the whole ugly story about what happened before she went to foster care. Then, she hung up on me. We hadn't spoken again.

I'd been desperate to talk to her again, but she didn't answer my calls or my texts that day. Now I understood why my mother hadn't filled in the blanks for me. Lucy—proud, strong as hell, independent as hell—wouldn't want anyone to know how vulnerable she'd been. She would've been infuriated to learn I'd heard the story from someone else. Hell, I had no doubt she was furious with herself for telling me. Then, we flew out to the middle of nowhere.

I knew it wasn't helpful, but I was frustrated. Even though my heart ached for how she felt and how her past had hurt her, it hurt to have her shut me out like this. She wasn't giving me a damn chance.

I heard the helicopter coming down to land not too far ahead. The smoke was thinning as the wind blew it away. Most of the crew was already waiting in the small, level clearing. I did a quick headcount, calculating that some of us would need to wait behind until Fred, or another pilot, could return later.

There was no way in hell all twenty of us could fit in that helicopter. I wondered if another helicopter was on its way. When we were this far out, we never knew which helicopters were being used solely to drop fire retardant and which could also be used for transport. All I focused on was whatever we needed to do to get the fire contained. We had contained it fairly well. The river should hold it, along with the wide firebreaks we'd established.

Cade's crew had been working on an opposite corner of the massive fire. He'd radioed with updates and should be meeting us here shortly.

Once he'd settled the helicopter to a landing, Fred climbed out and waved me over. His blue eyes crinkled at the corners with his smile and his gray hair was rumpled from the wind. After a quick greeting, he got right to business. "So who should I cart out first?" he asked.

I glanced to Jesse who gestured to a cluster of our crew sitting on the ground. They'd been the first to arrive here, so they'd done a full extra day of work. Weather had delayed the rest of us.

"Take as many as you can for now. I'll wait back with Jesse and the rest," I replied.

Fred nodded and turned away, calling to the crew. In short order, over half of our crew lifted up in the air with a wave from Fred. Jesse was planning to return to a location roughly a mile in and pick up some gear left behind after a firefighter on another crew had been injured. The crew hadn't been able to carry everything out when they needed to transport him. Nothing major, but he'd broken his ankle, so he certainly couldn't shoulder his heavy gear.

I settled in to wait, sipping water and hoping the weather would hold for the next few hours.

After a few minutes, I heard my name. I glanced over to see Cade approaching. Beck was at his side. Both of them looked pretty much the way I figured I did—their faces streaked with soot, their shoulders drooping from the weight of their gear, and their eyes weary.

They tossed their gear on the ground beside me and sat down. I handed a water bottle to Cade as Beck spoke.

"What's the schedule for the next helicopter?" he asked.

I looked up at the sky, clouds drifting against the blue backdrop as the smoke cleared. "Fred figured he'd be back for another pick up this evening. He said he'd radio after he checks on the schedule to see if there's another pilot who has room for a pick up."

I glanced beyond into the trees to see if anyone else was approaching. "Where's the rest of your crew?" I asked.

Cade drained his water bottle before answering. "They already left. We stayed behind last night. We helped Matt from the other crew get carried out, but left our gear in the process. So we headed back to pick it up this afternoon."

"Well, there's a small enough group left. We'll fit in one helicopter. Unless there's somebody else who's about to show up."

Cade chuckled and shook his head. "Nope. Just us."

We lapsed into quiet, resting against our bags. I was starting to wonder where Jesse was when my radio crackled. I tugged it off my bag. "Yeah?"

"Levi, we got a problem," Jesse said quickly.

"What's that?"

"I just got charged by a bull moose. You're not gonna fucking believe it, but I slipped and sprained my damn ankle."

Jesse sounded more annoyed than anything. Cade met my eyes and swore under his breath.

"How bad is it? I'll come meet you, but do I need to bring anybody with me?" I asked.

"I don't think so. I can't put much weight on it. As long as I'm not dealing with my gear and the chainsaw, I can limp along."

"And where's that moose?" I asked.

Jesse chuckled. "He bolted after I started up the chainsaw to scare him off."

"Okay, I'll be there in a bit."

I stood and glanced between Beck and Cade. "If Fred comes, radio me with a timeline. Looks like we can make it back before it's dark. I'll radio once we're on our way back."

With a wave, I turned to leave. For a moment, I considered leaving my gear behind. But that wasn't smart. My best guess was Jesse was about a mile in. Even though we had a good distance between the fire and us and the wind had shifted direction, I didn't want to be stupid.

The brief rest had been enough to rejuvenate me, so I hiked quickly. Being a hotshot firefighter meant being accustomed to grueling work and drawing energy out of empty reserves sometimes. It wasn't long before I reached Jesse. He was exactly where he told me he would be, propped on the ground with the chainsaw to his side and leaning on his bag of gear. He looked up with a grin when I reached him.

"Anything to get you to hike somewhere," he offered with a wink.

"How bad is your pain?" I asked with a chuckle.

He shrugged. "It's there. Nothing I can't manage."

Reaching down, I gripped his hand and assisted him to standing. He'd already put a brace on his ankle. I doubled up our gear bags on my shoulders and carried the chainsaw as we started to walk out.

Jesse's pace was slow, but steady. We'd maybe walked for about ten minutes when I felt the wind shifting again and the sound of hooves approaching from behind us. I glanced to Jesse.

"Please tell me that's not another moose," I commented, knowing perfectly well it was. I hadn't grown up roaming the wilderness of Alaska without knowing the distinct, rangy gait of a moose.

He caught my eyes and shrugged. "Probably is. Best bet is to run that chainsaw for a second."

Before I had a chance to do exactly that, three moose ran into our line of sight, including a rather irate looking bull moose with a massive set of antlers.

The bull moose paused in his pursuit of the two female moose, pawing the ground and snorting as he turned to face us through the trees.

I started up the chainsaw, but this time it didn't do a damn thing. The moose snorted again and took a few more strides in our direction. For the most part, moose weren't aggressive. The only exceptions were when you encountered a mother protecting her calves, bull moose during mating season, which was inconveniently now, and if you happened to startle one. They were near-sighted, so they often didn't see you approaching and could easily startle.

Spinning in a circle, I scanned the area. The moose was between us and where we needed to go. With Jesse's ankle in bad shape, we couldn't take a roundabout route. The landing area for the helicopters was roughly a half mile away directly ahead.

I radioed Cade. "Hey man, we're dealing with an annoyed moose. We're probably going to be late. If Fred gets there soon, no need to wait for us."

"I was about to radio as it is," Cade replied. "He radioed not long after you left. Another helicopter just landed. You sure you don't want us to wait?"

I glanced ahead at the moose. He was no

longer snorting and pawing the ground, but he hadn't moved yet.

"How long can the pilot wait?"

Cade's voice was muffled and then he returned. "He thinks about a half hour."

"Got it. I'll see if I can chase this guy off."

Signing off, I glanced to Jesse. We carried side arms whenever we were out in the backcountry. Not because we ever intended to shoot any animal, but the Alaskan wilderness came with some distinct dangers. In this area, grizzlies were the primary concern, moose secondary. Further north, there were polar bears, and further south, brown bears, the grizzly's larger cousins. At the moment, all we needed to do was get this bull moose to focus back on the ladies in his life.

Jesse nudged my shoulder. "Turn around, so I can snag my shotgun."

Turning, I glanced over my shoulder as he snagged his shotgun from where it was lashed onto his gear bag. "Hold off," I said.

He nodded. "Of course. I'm just gonna set off a warning shot."

Several warning shots later and a few more rips of the chainsaw, and it was clear this bull moose wasn't going anywhere, not for the time being. He'd settled in to nibble on some alders in the edge of the trees.

Chapter Thirty

LUCY

Snapping my mouth shut, I stared across the table at my mother. Feeling bad because I hadn't seen her in a few weeks, I'd invited her to meet me for coffee at Firehouse Café. She'd just shocked the hell out of me by commenting that she thought Levi was a nice guy. Beyond Amelia, I hadn't spoken to anyone about the fact anything was happening with Levi.

As my mind spun over the possibilities, I recalled Levi's mother was friends with her. I mentally sighed.

"Mom, Levi's just..."

I meant to say Levi was just a friend, but I couldn't bring myself to lie. I skipped past that. "I don't want to talk about men."

Okay, I hadn't meant to sound so ridiculous and uptight, but oh well. My point was clear.

My mother's blue eyes met mine, steady and calm. "I know. I think that's probably my fault."

Confused, I cocked my head to one side. "What do you mean?"

"Well, you had one role model for a relationship when you were growing up, and it was terrible. I'm not trying to be nosy about Levi. For what it's worth, I understand why you've kept your distance from me, and I'm at peace with it. The only reason I said anything about Levi was Gloria mentioned that she met you. She thinks you're lovely." My mother's lips curled at the corners with a slight smile. "In fact, she thinks Levi's in love with you."

My heart beat rapidly, like wings fluttering in my chest, the sound thundering through my ears. I wanted Levi to love me—so, so much.

Because I was foolishly in love with him. The depth of my feelings scared the hell out of me, and I'd been steeling myself to let him know I needed to move out. I planned to tell him when he got back. I hadn't left yet because I was taking care of Ham. That's right,

I was taking care of a hamster and that was my reason for staying when I knew every day I stayed put my heart more at risk. If I was being honest with myself, which I tried really hard not to be, my heart was already past the point of no return. I missed Levi so acutely, my heart physically ached.

This morning, I'd breathed in the scent of him on his sheets and wondered when I'd hear that his crew would be returning. I think even Maisie suspected something because I'd randomly called the station the other day and awkwardly managed to get in a question about when the crews were due back.

When I didn't reply to my mother, lost in my thoughts, she spoke again.

"I have so much respect for you. You're everything I wish I'd been able to be when I was younger and when I had you. It's no excuse, but I was only seventeen when I got pregnant. I had no idea what to do. All I knew was I loved you. Your father was who he was, he was violent and possessive and..." Her words trailed off, and she took a deep breath. "He was an asshole, and I wish like hell I'd been as strong as you are now and left him before you were even born."

Her words hit me so hard, I almost lost

my breath. I simply stared at her, rendered speechless.

If she sensed how stunned I was, she didn't comment on it. She continued, "You don't have to listen to anything I say. I love you, and I want the best for you. Every lesson you learned from your childhood made sense based on what happened. But most men aren't like your father. There are good men, and I would hope that you might give yourself a chance to have more than what I had. Levi's a good man. If he loves you the way his mother thinks he loves you, I would hope you would give him a chance. Not just for him, but for yourself."

I swallowed through the knot in my throat, emotion spiraling inside of me, a wild storm of feelings and confusion. My mother and I didn't talk like this. All these years since she moved up here with me, we'd had a polite, but distant relationship. Before that, the unspoken was the reality of life with my father. Though her actions spoke volumes, I'd never expected her to be this open about my childhood and the choices she had made before she finally broke free.

If she was aware of how flabbergasted I was, it didn't show. Her eyes were warm as she looked over at me.

"If I could do everything over, I would," she said softly.

I couldn't bring myself to speak yet and simply stared at her. After a moment, I managed to get the emotion barreling through me under control.

"I never thought you'd say that out loud," I finally said.

She took a sip of her coffee and nodded slowly. "I can see why. I was ashamed for a long time. I can't change the past, but I can change the future. I don't expect you to suddenly be close to me, but I'm going to try to be more honest with you. When Gloria told me about you and Levi, I was so happy. And then I got worried, worried you would be as strong as you are and not let anyone in. I don't expect you to let me in, but please don't shut everyone out."

Her words struck so close to home, it stung.

Somehow I got through the rest of our coffee break without having a full on meltdown in the middle of Firehouse Café. I even managed to give her a hug when I left.

That night, I lay in Levi's bed because like the foolish, lovesick girl I was, I couldn't bear not to sleep in his bed. I tried to will myself to find the resolve I needed to move past my feelings, but my willpower had dissolved into nothing. All I could think about was how much I missed him.

———

The following day, I arrived at the job site and was surprised when Amelia wasn't there. Usually, she arrived as early as I did. If not, she reliably called. When I called her, there was no answer. A sense of foreboding rose inside. Normally, I would just get to work, but my gut told me something was afoot. I turned my truck around and headed to our office.

Entering the office, I found Amelia sitting at her desk, architectural drawings scattered across the desk before her and her eyes damp with tears

"What's wrong?" I asked quickly.

"It's Cade. Their helicopter didn't make it to Fairbanks last night like it was supposed to," she said softly, her voice low and wooden.

My heart flew into my throat. A question flew out. "Do we know where Levi is?"

She shook her head slowly. "No. I just got off the phone, or I would've called you before."

I sank into the chair across from her,

scrambling for something to hold onto inside. My heart felt as if it were actually crack-
ing. My breath came in shallow bursts.

"What do we know?" I asked carefully.

"Everything I just told you," Amelia
replied, her eyes blank.

"Let's call Maisie," I said.

If anyone could scrounge up more information, Maisie could as the dispatcher for
Willow Brook Fire & Rescue.

I leaned over the desk, tapped the speakerphone button and dialed Maisie.

Maisie answered immediately. "I'm
guessing you're calling about Cade and Levi. I
was just about to call you two."

With my heart thudding and my gut
churning, I stared at the speaker, as if the
speakerphone itself could solve this entire
problem.

"What do you know?" I asked, looking
across at Amelia.

Maisie started talking quickly. "I just got
off the radio with Beck. He and Cade are
fine. I knew you'd be panicking, and I was
about to call you. The wind picked up yesterday evening, and it was getting dark because they waited too long for Jesse and Levi.
So they landed and camped out instead of
flying all the way to Fairbanks. The pilot ra-

dioed the update, but somehow no one called us here. They're already on their way in. Another helicopter is headed out to pick up Levi and Jesse, but no one's heard from them this morning."

On the heels of Amelia's sigh of relief, I promptly burst into tears.

"Lucy? Are you okay?" Maisie asked, sounding rightly confused.

Everything was crashing through me. I hadn't had the courage to tell Levi I loved him and I'd known it for days. Even worse, I'd had a meltdown in our last call and hung up on him. Now, I didn't even know where he was, or if he was safe.

Amelia gathered herself and quickly explained since all I could do was cry. "Uh, Lucy and Levi kinda have a thing."

"A thing?" Maisie asked.

"Yeah, and it's heavy." Amelia caught my eyes and shrugged. "I know I'm supposed to keep my mouth shut, but this is kind of important."

"It's okay," I managed in between sobs.

"Maisie, how soon can you find out where they are?" Amelia asked, steady and practical now that she knew Cade was safe.

Maisie spoke calmly, the voice I'd heard her use many times when I stopped by to visit her at the station. As the dispatcher, she was used to talking to people calmly no matter how upset they were. I'd never expected myself to be in this situation with her. She was my friend, and her even voice soothed my frayed nerves.

"We know precisely where they were when we last heard from them. It's just the reception is terrible there. We're guessing the battery on their radio died. I'm sure they're fine," she assured me.

I didn't hear much else while she and Amelia continued talking. Before I knew what was happening, Amelia gathered me up and was driving me out to Cade's parents house. I was simultaneously overwhelmed with emotion and numb, as if my internal circuits had overloaded. I didn't even realize where we were going until she pulled up in front of their home.

"What are we doing here?" I asked, glancing over to her.

"We're waiting with Cade's parents. It's a good place to wait because his dad's the police chief, so he'll get updates right away. He has a good friend up at Fairbanks Fire & Rescue," she explained.

I started to protest, but Amelia ignored me completely. I followed Amelia into the house, feeling out of sorts and embarrassed at how emotional I was.

Gloria and Brad were there. This should have surprised me, but it didn't. Willow Brook was small and everyone knew everyone. Cade's mother immediately thrust a cup of coffee in front of me and started making everyone breakfast.

Gloria reached over and gave my hand a squeeze, her grip warm and firm. Everyone was bustling around me in the kitchen with Cade's mother, Georgia, serving breakfast and coffee, while others chatted at the table and kitchen counter. Georgia insisted on serving me scrambled eggs and toast even though I only picked at my food. Cade's father, who also happened to be the police chief for Willow Brook, had called from the station to report that the locator beacon for Levi and Jesse was still active and precisely where they were expected to be.

Apparently, they didn't expect the helicopter to be able to get out to them until later this afternoon due to poor visibility. Rain had rolled through the area overnight, which was great news for the fire, but terrible news for getting an update soon. Everyone was assuming their radio batteries had died. Beyond the fact I felt as if a storm had lifted me up and slammed my heart broadside against a wall, I was annoyed that no one else seemed too rattled.

I discovered I had no idea, none whatsoever, what it was like for Amelia to have Cade out in the backcountry for weeks at a time. My stomach was churning, my heart felt heavy, and I was terrified.

Plain terrified. I desperately wanted to talk with Levi. More specifically, I wanted to erase our last conversation. Why, oh why, did I have to go and have that meltdown? It felt so childish now.

Now, all I wanted was a chance to tell him how I felt. I didn't even care if he didn't return my feelings.

I lifted my gaze to Gloria's and swallowed against the tight, achy feeling in my throat and chest. The sensation of emotion had moved past an abrupt tightness to a dull ache because it had been there for over an hour now.

Gloria gave my hand another squeeze before releasing it. "He'll be fine."

The confidence and firmness in her tone seemed ridiculous to me.

"How can you know that?" I asked.

Her eyes held mine, far too perceptive and far too knowing. "It's just a feeling. I'm not so silly as to think I can't be wrong. But I know my boy, and I don't have any sense he's not okay. He's about as resourceful as a man can get, and he's with Jesse who's just as resourceful. They'll be fine. You heard the update. They're outside of the area where the fire was contained and last night's rain helped in that regard. There's absolutely no way they would've walked back into the fire. They both have sidearms, so if anything were going to hurt them, they would've been able to dispatch it. I think they'll be fine because all of the information I have tells me they will."

The barest hint of a smile tugged at the corners of my mouth. I wanted to believe her. A tear rolled down my cheek, and she handed me a tissue.

"You sound so sure," I mumbled as I wiped my tears.

"It's confidence based on being practical," she offered. "Let's not think the worst. Certainly not when it isn't necessary."

She paused to take a sip of coffee, and I idly stirred my scrambled eggs with my fork. Gloria's voice broke through my hazy thoughts.

"I believe Levi's in love with you."

My heart started drumming inside my

chest again, as if hope itself was beating a drum.

"What makes you say that?" I asked.

Gloria had said as much to my mother, but I was curious to hear why she believed Levi loved me. Not to mention I was desperate to know.

She smiled softly and angled her head to the side. "Just the way he looks at you and the way he talks about you. I know my son well. He's a good man, and I don't say that because I'd like it to be true. He really is. You're the first woman he's ever brought over for dinner."

My surprise must've shown on my face because Gloria laughed.

"So you didn't know you had that place of honor? Absolutely. Levi's fairly private for the most part. He's dated here and there, but not once has he ever even mentioned a woman to me, and he's certainly never brought one home for dinner. Now don't go thinking that's the only reason I think he loves you. It's part of the equation because it tells me you mean something to him. The other part is I see how he looks at you and the way he is around you. He loves you."

I didn't realize my mouth had dropped open for a beat and snapped it shut when I did. Whether she expected me to say something in return or not, I didn't know. My words, pushy words, announced what I'd been hiding even from myself until this morning.

"I love him too," I blurted out suddenly. "Now I'm scared that something happened to him."

She held my gaze for a beat and nodded slowly. "It's rather terrifying, isn't it? Falling in love, I mean. I understand why you're worried right now. I am too, but I think he'll be okay. All the information that we have tells us he probably is. So hold on tight, and I'm pretty sure you'll be able to tell him that yourself."

Chapter Thirty-One

LEVI

A raven flew above us, calling loudly to another who returned its call from the trees. I dragged my sleeve across my face and glanced over to Jesse. We had successfully chased off the nosy moose yesterday evening. By that point, it was well past dusk and any chance to fly out for the night had passed us by. We'd set up camp for the night and were now waiting back at the clearing where a helicopter should arrive soon to pick us up. *Should* being the operative word here. Both of our radios were dead, in addition to our cell phones. My backup battery had lost its last bit of juice late last night.

Jesse was definitely in pain, but he was hanging in there. I was relieved his injury appeared to be minor. His ankle was swollen and bruised from where he slipped and jammed it against some rocks, but it was nothing more than a nasty sprain. We had plenty of ibuprofen to take the edge off of his pain.

I finished chewing my snack bar and caught his eye, handing him the thermos of coffee we were sharing. We were down to snack bars and freeze dried goods for food, but we had plenty of coffee left, so we'd made some with our camp stove.

"Any idea when they might make it?" I asked.

We'd camped where we were last night and walked the remaining half-mile or so to the clearing where the helicopter would hopefully pick us up soon. Jesse glanced at me as he took a swig of coffee and shrugged.

"Dunno. It was pretty cloudy this morning. Looks like it might clear enough this afternoon for them to fly out."

"How's that ankle?"

He shrugged again. "Eh, it hurts, but it could definitely be worse."

I pointlessly snagged my radio off the ground again. The battery had died at some point last night when I'd left it on by accident. Meanwhile, Jesse had dropped his in the river this morning. He'd fetched it out, but not before it shorted out from getting drenched.

I wondered if anyone was worried outside of our crew. I figured our crew likely wasn't too worried. They'd known we were set for the night. Lucy gave a wave in my thoughts. She was permanently lodged in my brain. Restless to get home and see her, I hoped like hell she missed me.

Through my disrupted hours of half-sleep last night, I'd let go of my frustration with her shutting me out. I knew what she'd shared with me had to have been hard for her. It wasn't as if I didn't understand why she was skittish. I needed to be patient because she was worth the wait.

I leaned against my gear bag, watching as the sun finally broke through the clouds. It had rained during the night, which should've given a good dousing to the fire. We could use a few more days of rain, although I'd take a few hours of clear skies to get out of here.

A raven called again from the trees nearby. Glancing over, I saw its dark form perched on a spruce tree. The fire hadn't reached this part of the forest, so the trees were still lush and green. The scent of the charred trees in the distance carried our way.

This fire had been burning for several weeks now. Fires burned like this in the summers out West. You'd only hear about them in the news when they were threatening communities, but they could burn for weeks in the Alaskan backcountry without a peep. We occasionally coordinated planned burns to manage areas.

The raven in question lifted from the trees and flew over near us, landing on the ground, maybe only ten feet away. I watched as it pecked at the ground, realizing it was likely feasting on some crumbs left from the guys yesterday. Half of our crew had hung out for a good bit before they'd been flown out, all of them tired, hungry, and chowing on whatever snacks they had left over.

The raven meandered closer. I watched curiously as two more ravens flew down to join in, clearly deciding Jesse and I were no threat. They busily cleaned up the crumbs we couldn't see. I adjusted my angle and looked out in the distance. It was beautiful out here. The sound of the nearby river running over the rocks soothed me. This part of the interior was a mix of rolling hills and flat tundra, the beauty stark. An eagle flew above, its call sharp and distinct.

I gulped in a deep breath of the clear,

chilly air, thinking a shower would be good about now. As a hotshot firefighter, I was used to going many days without much more than a dip in a river or lake, but once I knew we were close to civilization, I got impatient. At the moment, I was weary and anxious to see Lucy, hoping upon hope that she wasn't keeping her distance from me anymore.

———

A few hours later, I watched as the landscape rolled underneath me. Fred had flown in during a break in the clouds. The clouds were already thickening again. Fred expected we'd make it back to Fairbanks before the visibility was too low, for which I was damn relieved. Between wanting to get Jesse's ankle looked at and make sure he was comfortable and missing Lucy like crazy, I was ready to get closer to home.

Pulling my cell phone out, I glanced at the dead screen. This battery had lost its charge days ago. Fred had assured me he'd already radioed that we were safe. I wanted to talk to Lucy, but that wasn't happening. Not just yet. With a sigh, I put my phone away and leaned back in my seat, closing my eyes.

"Why are you pissed at your phone?" Jesse asked from the seat beside me.

Opening my eyes, I rolled my head to the side and caught his curious gaze. "Just hoping to call my parents and Lucy."

He looked confused and then his gaze cleared. "Oh yeah, she's been staying with you. Well, we'll be in Fairbanks soon. You can call there."

I didn't know what look passed across my face, but he arched a brow. "I think I missed something. Is Lucy more than a friend?"

For a beat, I considered not saying anything. Fuck it. I wasn't going to keep hiding everything.

"She might be more than a friend. Actually she is," I finally said. "Here's hoping she sees it that way too."

Jesse smiled slowly and chuckled. "Lucy Caldwell, now she's a tough one."

"Trust me, I know," I replied, my mind spinning back to our last conversation.

I rolled my head to look back out the window, watching as the trees disappeared beneath us and the mountains near Fairbanks came into view. Our helicopter touched down shortly thereafter. Inside of a few minutes, we were being hustled into the station. I checked in with my crew first, made sure

Jesse was set up with the medical team and then hunted down Cade, not even bothering to say hello when I reached his side.

"Can I borrow your phone?" I asked.

At his look of confusion, I explained, "Mine's so dead, I can't even make a call on it right now."

He chuckled and handed his over. "Let me guess, you're calling Lucy. She's at my parents' place with Amelia. I already called over and let everyone know you're fine."

I barely absorbed what he said as I tapped in Lucy's number. The phone rang once, and she answered right away.

"Hello," she said, her tone choppy.

"Hey babe."

"Levi?" she asked, her voice lilting at the end, my name coming out rushed and almost frantic.

So damn happy she wasn't pissed that I called her babe, I laughed. "Of course, who did you think it was?"

"Well, this isn't your number. And why are you laughing? I've been scared to death."

"Hey, I thought you knew I was okay. Cade told me he called Amelia."

All of the sudden, Lucy—tough Lucy who almost never let down her guard—burst into tears.

She cried with as much gusto as she'd told me to fuck off once upon a time. Her tears derailed me into silence for a moment.

I finally scrambled my thoughts together. "Lucy, are you okay?"

"No! I'm not okay, and it's all your fault," she said in between sniffles and messy breaths. "I love you, and..." Her words stopped with another loud sob.

"Lucy, Lucy," I finally said. My heart felt as if it would burst, and I couldn't quite believe she'd said what I thought she said.

"What?" she asked in return.

I heard a muffled sound and then her blowing her nose, rather loudly. "Sorry, I needed to blow my nose," she explained, her breath was coming in short little gasps.

"Did I hear you right?" I asked after moment of silence.

"Which part?"

"The I love you part. Because I love you, so..."

She hiccupped and then burst into tears. Again.

"You heard me right, I love you," she managed between breathy heaves and more sniffles. "I'm sorry I got all weird. I'm just so happy you're okay. I was going to be really mad at the world if you weren't." She took a shaky breath, and I could feel her thinking through the phone. "I kinda dumped some heavy stuff the last time we talked. If you want to talk about it..."

"We don't have to talk about anything unless you want to. I can't say I'm glad you hung up on me, but I'm glad you told me everything. Let's just focus on now for now. We'll have plenty of time for talking later."

She was quiet for a beat before the sound of a soft sigh filtered through the phone. "Okay. I miss you. When will you be home? I think Ham misses you too."

I chuckled, my heart feeling so full, I thought it might burst. I was filthy, exhausted and hundreds of miles away from her, but I was happy.

I wished like hell she were right here with me.

"When will you be home?" she repeated.

"I don't know yet," I said with a chuckle.

Normally, I'd already know. I hadn't even bothered to check in to find out if my crew was scheduled to return to the fire site, or if we'd be heading home soon. I glanced over to Cade who was still standing nearby. "Hey, do you know our return schedule yet?" I called over.

Cade shook his head. I returned to Lucy. "As soon as I know, I'll call you, okay?"

Someone called my name, and I glanced over my shoulder to see the superintendent from one of the other crews waving me over.

"I gotta go, Lucy. You okay?"

"Uh huh. I'm fine. I just got overwhelmed," she said with a sniffle.

It nearly tore me up to hear her cry, and I hated I wasn't with her now.

"In case you were worried, I've taken very good care of Ham," she said with a sniffly laugh.

I needed that laugh, if only because it let me know she was okay. I chuckled. "I wasn't worried. You spoil him worse than me with the carrots."

That got another laugh from her. "Okay. I guess you have to go."

I held tight to the phone because I didn't want to end this call. Cade nudged me on the shoulder. "I do. I'll call when I have our schedule." I paused, considering whether to say the words I wanted. They slipped out on their own. "Miss you."

For a moment, I didn't think she would reply, but she did. "Me too. Call me."

———

Three long days later, I climbed into my car at the station, anxious to get home and see Lucy. The world had not followed my wishes. I'd wanted to fly home the same day we landed in Fairbanks, but it was a no go. They had our crew wait in case we needed to be sent out for another rotation. Though I knew it made sense given the travel logistics, I'd been chafing at the bit the whole damn time. The rain had been on my side though and put a damper on the fire, cutting the wait short. I hadn't even known until this morning what time we were due to fly out.

A short drive later, my heart started drumming the moment I saw Lucy's truck parked in front of the house. I rolled to a quick stop and was jogging up the stairs within seconds. When I opened the door, she was leaning over looking inside the oven. The sight of her lush bottom greeted me.

My cock stood at attention instantly. Much as I wanted her bare and tangled up with me, more than that I wanted to hold her close and just absorb the feel of her. She jumped when the door clicked shut. Spinning around, her eyes widened and a smile claimed her lips. Her hair was in a messy ponytail, and she had on an apron with a moose on it.

Her breath hitched as I strode to her,

closing the distance between the door and where she stood inside of a second. I stopped inches from her. Her sky blue eyes were wide, her cheeks were flushed and her lips, fuck me, her lips could bring me to my knees.

I didn't wait anymore, dipping my head and catching her delectable lips with mine. I meant for this to be a slow greeting. Our kiss started slow, her mouth opening for me on a sigh. The moment her tongue tangled with mine, I was done for.

I growled, sliding my palm down her spine, tangling my other hand in her hair and cupping her sweet bottom to tug her firm against me. I shoved her apron up out of the way and yanked her leggings down. Reaching between her thighs, I cupped her over her thin cotton panties. I could feel the wet heat of her desire. She moaned and tore her lips free of mine.

"Levi..." she gasped.

"Mmm," I murmured as I dragged my tongue along the side of her neck.

Spinning us around, I took a step, lifting her up and sliding her hips on the counter. Leaning back, I caught her eyes. "I missed you."

She held my gaze, the moment electric. Lifting a hand, she traced my lips. "I missed you too." She took a deep breath and then grinned slowly. "Now let's get these out of the way," she said as she yanked at the buttons of my jeans and shoved my shirt up.

In a matter of seconds, we were both nearly bare, and I was lifting her back onto the counter, her panties discarded.

With the feel of her palm curling around my cock and my heart thudding hard and fast against my ribs, lust was pounding through me so hard I could barely think.

I forced myself to hold still. My desire for Lucy was so powerful, I could hardly withstand it. Its force was akin to a river, running wild through the mountains. The sheer, raw power of it was what drew me to her from the start. Yet, it wasn't simply that which bound me to her. It was our connection, the shimmering web of intimacy that spun us tighter and tighter together whenever I was close to her like this.

My mind flashed back to before when she was always brushing me off, her sky blue eyes flashing with desire and anger at once as she tried to keep me at bay. When she let go, that blue darkening like the sky in a storm. Once in a while, vulnerability flickered in the depths when she let her guard down.

As she held my gaze, her breath hitched,

and I could see her pulse fluttering in her neck, her skin flushed with need. She curled her legs around me, sliding her palm up and down my cock. I was so hard, the pressure was almost unbearable. I reached up, brushing a loose tendril of hair away from her face and dipping my head to catch her lips in a kiss again.

Only then did I reach between her thighs again, stroking through her slick folds. When I drew back, she gasped my name, her hips rocking impatiently against me. Gripping my cock in my fist, I dragged it back and forth, coating it with her juices.

Her eyes flashed. "Stop teasing," she ordered, nudging her hips into mine.

Obediently, I followed her order and sank into her deeply. Her creamy clench welcomed me, hot and slick. I groaned, almost coming instantly. Forcing myself to hold still, I dipped my head to catch my breath in the curve of her neck, breathing in her musky scent.

"I love you," I murmured gruffly, lifting my head.

Her eyes widened, and I felt her pulse kick up a notch where my hand rested along her collarbone.

Chapter Thirty-Two

LUCY

The rich blue of Levi's gaze held me. I couldn't look away as my pulse thundered, echoing through my entire body. His words struck me at my core. For a beat, anxiety bloomed inside, an anxiety I knew well. I managed a breath, holding his gaze, and felt myself relax. He held still, his cock stretching me. Connected as deeply as we could physically be, it felt as if we were one.

"I love you too," I finally said. I might've said the words more than once already, but they were still fresh.

He answered with his lips, catching mine in a soft kiss. He drew his hips back and then sank into me deeply, the stretch delicious and overwhelming. I was so close to the edge already, I clung to the moment. I didn't want this to end too quickly.

The blunt truth was I'd gotten rather accustomed to finding release with him. It had been two long weeks apart. I'd missed him acutely—physically and emotionally. The internal storm of my emotions heightened every sensation. My body was frantic with pure, raw, primal need.

Feeding into my need was the intimacy curling like smoke in the heat of our desire. With every stroke, pleasure spun through me, spinning tighter and tighter until he reached between us, pressing his thumb over my clit. My release hit me so hard, I shouted his name, pleasure sending me flying apart in his arms.

I distantly heard him crying my name and the heat of his release filling me as he went taut. On a low groan, he relaxed against me, his head falling into the curve of my neck with his breath gusting against my shoulder. I breathed in the scent of him, the woodsy, crisp, masculine scent he carried with him.

"Your sheets don't hold a candle to the real thing."

I hadn't meant to speak my thoughts aloud, but the words slipped out. He lifted his head, his eyes catching mine.

"What about my sheets?"

I flushed all over, but I was relaxed in his arms with his warm, teasing gaze holding mine. "Your sheets don't smell as good as you," I said simply.

He chuckled and then lifted me, holding me against him and still buried inside of me, as he walked us upstairs into the shower.

LUCY

A few weeks later, I stood in Levi's kitchen and glanced over to where he sat at the kitchen table with Ham sitting on his shoulder. He did this with Ham often, feeding him little bits of lettuce and carrots. A smile tugged at the corners of my mouth as I bit back the urge to laugh.

It was ridiculous really. Levi—hotshot firefighter, sexy as hell, tough as hell, and too handsome for his own good—carefully offering snacks to a small brown and white hamster. Snagging my phone off the counter, I quickly snapped a photo.

"I'm sending that to Maisie," I offered with a grin.

He chuckled. "So?"

"She can share with your crew. You look ridiculous, you know."

He shrugged, entirely unabashed. "Ham likes to get his snacks this way."

"I know." My heart suddenly felt full. Restless, I spun away, emotion hitting me in waves. These little episodes, where I felt caught in a riptide of emotion, had been happening a lot lately. I didn't quite know what to do with any of it.

I might've been able to admit that I loved Levi, but I wasn't used to this. For my whole life, I'd been fending for myself one way or another. Now, here I was still at Levi's, still trying to figure out what to do next.

I spoke over my shoulder. "I think I found a place to rent," I said.

The moment I spoke, my heart did that funny little tumble. Relieved there were a few dishes in the sink, I turned on the water and started washing them.

After a beat, he spoke. "Come here."

I turned the water off and dried my hands on the dishtowel before turning to face Levi. He lifted Ham off of his shoulder and carefully set him on the floor. Beckoning me with his hand, his eyes held mine. Since I couldn't have willed my body not to respond even if I wanted to, I was crossing the room to him before I even thought about it. When I reached him, he took the towel out of my hand and set it on the table, tugging me between his knees.

His gaze was somber and intent. In a flash, the air was shimmering with the electricity and intimacy that simply existed between us. It was its own force, one that could not be denied.

He hooked a finger in one of my belt loops. I was wearing a faded pair of jeans and a t-shirt. He lifted his other hand and traced my brow, his fingertip trailing down along my cheek.

His touch was like a blaze of fire on my skin. Emotion welled inside of me again, and he hadn't said another word yet.

"What?" I asked, my voice thick. Tears wicked up from the knot of emotion in my throat, and I couldn't will them away. I felt the heat of a tear rolling down my cheek and his thumb brushing it away.

"What's wrong?" he asked, his tone gruff.

I shook my head sharply. "I don't know. Why are you looking at me like that?"

Wiping the next tear that fell with his thumb, his gaze never wavered. "I understand why you might want to have your own place, but..." He paused, taking a deep breath.

"You're it for me. I'll be patient if I have to, but I wish you would stay here."

I stared at him, my heart beating wildly and the achy feeling easing inside. Wordlessly, I nodded. I took a deep breath, the tension bundled inside starting to loosen. I was stubborn, really stubborn, and I knew it. I thought back to a comment Amelia had made the other day. I'd said something to the effect that it had been easy for her to decide Cade was the one because he'd always been the one for her, and there was no compromise.

She'd eyed me and shook her head. "There's always a compromise. I think you've forgotten how proud and stubborn I can be. I had to let go of a lot of anger. It didn't matter whether it was rational or not. It's always easier to be alone. Because then you don't have to be vulnerable, you don't have to put your own heart on the line."

I'd turned her words over in my mind like a worry stone, again and again, evaluating them from every angle. In the end, she was right, and I knew it.

So I stared at Levi, realizing he was putting his heart on the line for me, and I wasn't doing the same. Oh, I loved him, and I wanted him. Yet, I was clinging to making decisions that were all about me, while hedging my bets on us.

On the heels of another deep breath, I reached up to brush a lock of his hair away from his forehead, that tawny golden hair that I loved so.

"Okay, I'll stay," I said softly, my heart beating wildly and soaring.

His smile was like the sun coming out behind the clouds. He dropped his hand from my cheek. With his chin just about level with mine, he angled his head and dropped a kiss on my neck.

"Oh thank God. I didn't want to beg," he said with a low laugh.

·····································

EPILOGUE

·····································

Levi

One year later

Lucy stood in front of me. We were standing outside of Firehouse Café on a chilly, early autumn evening. We had just arrived at a surprise party planned by Amelia, Susannah, and Maisie. All of this planning had taken place behind Lucy's back.

We'd gotten married the day before. Lucy's blonde hair was piled up in a messy knot, the wind blowing it wild. She had absolutely, positively refused to plan a wedding, so we'd eloped.

Well, I didn't know if it was technically eloping when we told everyone we were doing just that. I loved Lucy, so much that I still wondered how I'd ever lived without her.

But trying to get to the actual marrying part hadn't been easy. She'd dragged her feet every step of the way. She didn't want a ceremony, and she refused to wear a wedding dress. The only part she hadn't argued about was getting married. Thank fuck for that.

With the help of friends, I'd managed to get her here. Cade had done a bit of dirty work by swapping out her truck battery for a dead one while she and Amelia were working today. Orchestrating the plan, Amelia had conveniently left work early, so Lucy was stuck at the job site and had to call me for a ride.

We already had 'plans' to meet Amelia and Cade for dinner at Wildlands. I claimed I needed to stop and pick up something from Janet at the café. We reached the door, at which point Lucy realized it said *Closed*.

She peeked through the window before spinning back to face me. "Why is it closed and *only* our friends are there? And your parents? And my mom?" she demanded, hands on her hips as she glared at me.

"Amelia wanted to have a party since you wouldn't let her plan our wedding," I offered, reaching for her hand and reeling her to me. "So here's the party."

She stared at me for a moment and then

shook her head, her cheeks flushing. She relaxed against me, burying her face in my chest.

"Why does everyone have to make it a *thing*? I hate when people pay attention to me," she mumbled into my chest.

I smoothed a hand over her hair, tucking a lock behind her ear and cupping her chin. Nudging it up, I looked down at her. "Because people love you. We have dinner with friends and family all the time. That's all this is."

Her teeth snagged her bottom lip as she eyed me. On the heels of a sigh, she murmured, "Fine. Let's go in."

———

A few hours later, after plenty of food had been served and probably a bit too much alcohol, Lucy was sitting on my lap at one of the tables. We'd just been trounced in poker by Maisie. She was epically good at poker, so this was a common occurrence.

Lucy swung her legs, one of her heels bumping my calf, and looked to me. Her cheeks were flushed, and her eyes bright. She was so damn beautiful, I lost my breath for a beat.

"We always lose. Why do we keep doing this?" she asked as she traced her fingers idly along my forearm.

I still wasn't quite accustomed to how easily she affected me. The light touch of her fingertips on my arm—my arm for crying out loud—and I was half-distracted. I forced my attention to her question.

"Because it's fun," I replied with a chuckle, catching her hand in mine.

She laughed and glanced to Maisie. "Someday I'll beat you."

At that moment, Lucy's mother paused by the table. Lucy looked up at her mother. "Are you leaving?"

"Oh yes. You know me, I like to get to bed early," Jody replied.

Lucy slipped off my lap and gave her mother a hug. They'd come to more of a relaxed peace over the last year.

After Lucy hugged her mother goodbye, she slipped back into my lap and glanced over at Maisie, picking up where she'd left off. "It's a good thing we don't play for money. At this point, you'd have enough for a down payment on a house."

Maisie laughed, while Beck flashed a grin and sifted his fingers through the curls on Maisie's shoulder. It was beyond nice—the feeling of relaxing with Lucy and our friends.

Cade said something, but I wasn't paying attention. Rather, I'd gotten distracted by Lucy's musky scent and was dusting kisses along the side of her neck. The taste of her skin was a straight shot of lust to my groin.

"Levi?" Cade asked, just loud enough to remind me we were in public.

I glanced his way. "Oh, were you talking to me?"

He rolled his eyes. "I was."

"Need something?" I asked.

"Just asked if you'd like the good battery back."

Lucy's fist thumped my shoulder. "I knew something was up with my battery! I just had it replaced a few months ago."

"Hey, that wasn't my plan. It was Amelia's idea."

"Absolutely. I knew if Levi wasn't driving, you'd never stop here. I have no shame," Amelia said firmly.

Lucy threw a balled up napkin at Amelia, her eyes catching mine again.

"It wasn't so bad, was it?" I asked.

She held my gaze, and for a flash, everything else fell away. We might as well have been alone. The air hummed around us as she shook her head slowly. "No, it wasn't bad at all." She dipped her head, dropping a kiss at the base of my neck. "It's all worth it because I love you," she murmured.

And then I was kissing her, our tongues tangling. I truly forgot where we were until the voices around us punctured my haze.

I drew back, thinking I needed to get her out of here as soon as feasibly possible. I needed her bare naked and skin to skin with me.

"I can't believe you ever teased me for being whipped," Cade said.

I glanced to him and shrugged nonchalantly. I was far past giving a damn that anybody knew I'd do anything for Lucy.

Lucy said something to Amelia and then settled against me. Her gaze canted up to mine, her sky blue eyes taking my breath away.

"Should we go?" she asked.

"Let's."

I pulled her close, catching her lips in a kiss. I stood, lifting her with me, and carried her out in my arms—into the late summer night with stars scattered like diamonds across the plum colored sky.

———

Thank you for reading Burn So Bad - I hope you loved Lucy & Levi's story!

For more smoking hot firefighter romance, Susannah & Ward's story is up next in Hot Mess. An epic second chance romance between two people who weren't looking for love. "Oh lord this book was so good there aren't enough stars to rate it. Five will have to do. Epic read." Don't miss Ward's story!

Keep reading for a sneak peek!

Be sure to sign up for my newsletter for the latest news, teasers & more! Click here to sign up: http://jhcroixauthor.com/subscribe/

WARD

I stared across the room, unable to keep my eyes off of Susannah Gilmore. She was leaning against the polished wooden bar, her strawberry blonde hair spilling out in a mass of curls around her shoulders. I didn't know what the hell the bartender was saying to her, but I was instantly annoyed. The look in his eyes was one of blatant appreciation.

Not that I blamed him. Susannah was fucking gorgeous. Strong as hell, feisty as hell, and so damn sexy, it was a miracle I'd managed to keep my hands to myself the last few days.

I was in Willow Brook, Alaska to meet the hotshot firefighter crew I was about to join as superintendent. I was only here for one more night before returning to visit my mother. I'd almost rescheduled this trip because the original plan had been for me to start this week. That was before my mother was moved into hospice care earlier this week.

In the meantime, I intended to do one thing before I left for the month tomorrow morning—have another night with Susannah, a repeat of our last night when we both finished our hotshot training in California four years ago. That night was seared into my memory. I hadn't known what to expect when I learned she worked on the crew I'd be leading.

Four years was long enough for both of us to forget each other. Yet, I'd stepped into the station here and known she was in the room before I even saw her. My body was a tuning fork tuned solely to her. I'd been here for three days since, and the lust simmered on high the entire time. We couldn't be around each other without practically catching on fire.

I knew pursuing her wasn't smart. Hell, I

was about to become her boss. Yet, I didn't particularly want to think smart right now. I wanted to forget everything else, and Susannah could help me do that.

I watched as the bartender turned away from Susannah to serve another customer. The crew had brought me with them to Wildlands Bar & Lodge, apparently a popular place, judging by how crowded it was. It was late, and most of the crew had left for the night. When it was clear the bartender was keeping busy, I took that moment to make my approach.

Leaning against the bar beside Susannah, I glanced to her. Simply being close to her, my body tightened further and my cock twitched. She didn't have to do a fucking thing to turn me on. All she had to do was exist.

Her blue eyes caught mine as she looked over, a pink flush staining her cheeks.

"Ward, I thought you'd left for the night," she said.

I leaned on the bar with both elbows, if only to mask my aching arousal. Shaking my head, I held her rich blue gaze. "Not yet."

We stared at each other, the air humming around us, snapping and crackling with electricity. A few years back I'd been called up to help with a fire in the backcountry here in Alaska. I'd heard stories about the eruption of Mount Augustine back in the nineteen-eighties. According to a fellow firefighter I met, the ash had been thick, and it occasionally formed small clouds in the air where the particles from the volcano rubbed against each other, creating a mini electrical storm within the clouds.

I'd never seen anything like that myself, but the memory of it stuck with me. That was what it felt like when I was near Susannah.

She didn't say a word, but she didn't look away either. Her tongue darted out, swiping across her bottom lip.

After a moment, she spoke. "We're gonna have to figure this out."

"Figure what out?" I asked.

Her breath drew in sharply. I took the moment to just soak her in. She had freckles scattered across her porcelain cheeks, and her nose tipped up at the end. She was so damn gorgeous and endearing at once with this tomboy vibe I loved. I couldn't say why she hit me so hard. Hell, it wasn't as if I hadn't met other beautiful women. There weren't many female firefighters, yet she wasn't a complete anomaly. For me, she was. One look at her, and it was like a swift kick straight to my gut and my heart. She was a living, breathing shot of adrenaline and lust in my veins.

I understood her question. The bald truth was I was about to become the superintendent for her crew. As one of the crew foremen, she would answer directly to me once I was in my official capacity. Although I knew the reasoning behind her question, I wanted to make her say it. Because I wasn't in my official position yet and wouldn't be until I returned. I wasn't above admitting that the knowledge I'd be her boss only made me want her more. The fact our attraction shouldn't be happening only fed into its fire.

Susannah lifted her chin, not backing down or looking away. "You're taking over as superintendent for my crew. We need to forget about that night."

I held her gaze and shook my head slowly. "You can't make me forget anything, and I know you haven't forgotten either. In fact, I think maybe we should have another night like that. Tonight."

Her lips parted and her breath hissed through her teeth. I suppose she expected me to be proper. Fuck that. I knew who and what I wanted. Her. Bare naked and tangled up with me.

Her eyes darkened as she stared at me. For a moment, I thought she was going to tell me to fuck off, but she didn't. She nodded, just barely.

Snagging her drink off the bar, she downed it quickly. "Follow me."

"Lead the way," I replied.

She spun away, her cowboy boots striking on the hardwood floor as she strode quickly in front of me, her hips swinging with every step.

SUSANNAH

I could feel the heat of Ward's gaze on me as I walked ahead of him. I threaded my way through the tables, barely registering the hum of voices around us. The bar was crowded, yet we might as well have been alone in a room. I turned into the hallway at the back, not waiting to see if he was behind me. My body knew he was with certainty. The air around us snapped with the force of the attraction between us. Any hopes I had that this yearning, burning fire between us would have dissipated had been dashed the moment he walked into the station the other day.

Ward Taylor had somehow managed to become even more attractive than the last time I'd seen him. I didn't know if that was a factual observation, but that was sure as hell how my body felt. Black curls, always slightly tousled, and those silver gray eyes, like the sky on a stormy summer day. One look from him, and it seared through me. His body was honed to perfection. I'd thought myself immune to men like him. As a hotshot firefighter, I spent my days with men in their physical prime. Yet, not a single man affected me the way Ward did.

Ward carried himself with an edge of danger, quiet strength, and simmering power under the surface. Back when I trained with him, he kept his distance from all of us. Oh, he was a good teammate, but there was a part of him that he kept under wraps. I sensed something or someone had hurt him. I'd never scratched beneath the surface to understand more.

Despite trying damn hard to erase it from my memory, I'd never forgotten the night we'd had together. It was so far and above any other sexual experience I'd ever had, I couldn't imagine anything coming close.

Three days with him around the station, passing by each other like flint to stone again and again—each pass striking another spark into the fire that just wouldn't die.

I'd been obsessing about how to handle the fact he was about to become my boss, while I nearly melted at his feet every time we were anywhere near each other. A respite was on the horizon because Ward was leaving for a month since his mother was sick. Cade and Levi were going to help out until Ward could return. That was what they been doing all along since Al's retirement.

As it was, we had one cranky as hell crew member who was flat pissed he hadn't gotten the job of superintendent. The rest of us on the crew had been relieved. Chad was an asshole. As far as I was concerned, Al should've fired him, but he hadn't. Ward was going to inherit that problem, although I felt like he was better suited to deal with it than our last superintendent.

Ward took no bullshit. It was all business at all times out in the field, and that was what we needed. Sad as I was to learn his mother was in hospice, even though Ward barely showed any emotion over it, it gave me some breathing room to figure out what the hell to do.

Yet right now, tonight, I was doing the craziest thing I could imagine. The moment Ward walked over and looked at me, I was a goner. I wanted him so fiercely. I was flat crazy for giving into it, but my need for him was rushing through me with such force, I couldn't ignore it. I was busy telling myself we could do this and then move on.

I knew little of Ward's personal life. He had a few friends when we were in training together. He was quiet and bordered on brooding. Unlike some of the other guys who liked to party and have a good time, he laid low. He certainly didn't do romance. In fact, our epic one-night stand had started with him pointing out it was perfect because we would never see each other again.

I couldn't even contemplate what he thought tonight might mean. As I walked down the hallway, which felt like forever, I could already feel the slick moisture soaking my panties. Just thinking about the memory of him sinking into me, every hard, thick inch of him, was enough to make me wild.

Ward knew how to use his hands, his lips, and his tongue so well, he'd left me boneless. He'd acquainted himself with every inch of my body, including my now dripping wet pussy, before fucking me until I forgot where I ended and he began.

Maybe one more round with him would burn my need to ashes.

As I passed by the restroom, I paused, turning to see him behind me. He ambled, his long stride eating up the distance between us with little effort.

"I'm going to use the restroom really quick, okay?"

His eyes burned through the distance between us as he nodded. He stopped in the hallway as I stepped inside, leaning against the door to catch my breath.

I didn't need to go to the bathroom, but I needed a moment to get a grip. I stared at myself in the mirror. My hair was a bit wild tonight, and my cheeks were flushed. I had a full body flush just from Ward's presence. Taking a deep breath, I splashed cool water on my face and washed my hands. My body was nearly humming in anticipation.

When I stepped out, Ward was leaning against the wall across from the door, one hand hooked in his pocket and the other hanging loose at his side. He wore faded black jeans, battered leather black boots, and a navy T-shirt that outlined his sculpted chest and broad shoulders. My mouth went dry and my pulse took off, skittering wildly.

My breath came in shallow pants and my sex clenched as I stared at him. Perhaps two feet separated us. From across the hallway, he reached out and hooked his finger in my belt loop, pulling me flush against his body inside of a quick breath.

I liked to think of myself as a woman in control of her life, of her destiny, of her body and her mind. Most of the time, I was.

Except when it came to Ward. All of my defenses burned to nothing in the searing heat of his presence.

When my body bumped against his, I almost moaned aloud. I hadn't forgotten how good he felt—all hard strength, coiled energy and power. Even his face was strong with a square jaw, sculpted cheekbones, the dark slash of his brows over those silver gray eyes, and a nose that looked if it had been broken once, giving him a roguish charm.

Ward wasn't much for smiling, which made it dangerous when he did. Like now. His lips curled at one corner with his eyes locked to mine.

My breath caught and my belly clenched.

He didn't say a word. One hand slid around to cup my bottom and pull me tight against him, the hard ridge of his arousal pressing into my belly and sending a gush of moisture into my panties. I didn't know if it was actually possible to orgasm simply from standing beside someone, but if anyone could make that happen, Ward could.

He lifted his other hand, brushing a loose curl off my cheek and tucking it behind my ear. Goose bumps ran in a shiver down my side.

I could barely breathe, my body pulsing with anticipation. In a flash, he claimed my mouth with his. He kissed as boldly as I remembered, his hand palming my ass as he rocked his arousal into me, hard and insistent at the apex of my thighs.

Kissing him was like getting caught inside of a flame. His hand tangled roughly in my hair as he devoured my mouth. Deep sweeps of his tongue, drawing back to nip at my bottom lip. Inside of a matter of seconds, I was so caught up in our kiss, I completely forgot where we were, nudged out of my madness only when I heard the door to the hallway open from the parking lot.

My panties were drenched and my breath came in rough gasps. I broke free and stumbled away from him. My gaze swung wildly to the back doorway to see a cluster of people I didn't recognize entering. Thank God. The chances it could be someone I knew were high. I'd been born and raised in Willow Brook and knew most everyone local. But it was early spring, and the tourists were already crowding into town.

The group filed down the hallway between Ward and I. His eyes never left mine, my gaze drawn back to his like a magnet. The force of his gaze was so powerful, it felt as if he were actually touching me. After the customers made their way past us, their footsteps echoing on the hardwood floor and the sounds from the bar filtering into the hallway, he reached across the space between us again, catching my hand and reeling me close.

My brain tried to fire off a thought. But it was as if all of the signals were crossed, haywire in the heat of the desire between us. Flush against him again, my nipples tight, need pounding inside of me, and my breath barely under control, I couldn't manage a word.

"Let's go," he said, his gruff voice sending a prickle down my spine.

I nodded wordlessly. He turned, my hand held tight in his. I suddenly remembered what it felt like to be held by him—beyond the pounding need, there was more. This man, so handsome, so sexy he was dangerous, somehow made me feel safe. Though there was a distance to him, a wall I didn't know how to scale, I felt safer with him than I'd ever felt with anyone in my life.

SUSANNAH

One month later

The little blue line stared at me, distinct and clear. There were three of them sitting in front of me on the bathroom counter. Three blue lines, all telling me the same thing. I had a fourth pregnancy test with me. Maybe I was crazy, but I wanted to be sure. Plus, I liked the number four, it was nice and even. I pulled the last test out of the box. With my heart pounding and anxiety spinning through me, I was almost sweating. I squatted over the toilet again—another undignified moment where I tried to direct my pee onto the little plastic stick.

Tugging my underwear and leggings up again, I looked at the test immediately, watching as the distinct blue line appeared. I still couldn't quite absorb the fact that I now had four drug store pregnancy tests telling me I was pregnant. My mind tumbled wildly, thoughts racing through as I scrambled to make sense of this.

I can't be pregnant. This has to be a mistake.

Coming soon!
Hot Mess

Go here to sign up for information on new releases: http://jhcroixauthor.com/subscribe/

5) Follow me on Instagram at https://www.
instagram.com/jhcroix/
6) Like my Facebook page at https://www.
facebook.com/jhcroix

Into The Fire Series
Burn For Me
Slow Burn
Burn So Bad
Hot Mess
Burn So Good
Sweet Fire
Play With Fire
Melt With You
Burn For You
Crash & Burn
Swoon Series
This Crazy Love
Wait For Me
Break My Fall
Brit Boys Sports Romance
The Play
Big Win
Out Of Bounds
Play Me
Naughty Wish
Diamond Creek Alaska Novels

When Love Comes
Follow Love
Love Unbroken
Love Untamed
Tumble Into Love
Christmas Nights
Last Frontier Lodge Novels
Take Me Home
Love at Last
Just This Once
Falling Fast
Stay With Me
When We Fall
Hold Me Close
Crazy For You
Just Us
Catamount Lion Shifters
Protected Mate
Chosen Mate
Fated Mate
Destined Mate
A Catamount Christmas
Ghost Cat Shifters
The Lion Within
Lion Lost & Found

ACKNOWLEDGMENTS

I love the journey of every story, and this one was no exception. Lucy & Levi stole my heart. If you've read any of my other books, you probably know I love writing strong women. Lucy was such a contradiction, and an absolute joy to write - so strong and sassy, yet vulnerable underneath. Many thanks to my editor, Laura Kingsley, for giving it to me straight and making sure I did right by Lucy & Levi.

Yoly Cortez created more magic with this cover, and it's purple - my favorite! My proofreader angels - Janine, Beth P., Terri D., Terri E., & Heather H. - thank you so much!

My readers - I thank you with every story, and I'll never stop. Thank you from the bottom of my heart for taking a chance on my books, for your fabulous messages, and for making this more fun than I ever could have imagined.

Last, but never least, DBC for sharing this crazy journey called life. Oh, and my dogs who make me run every day with them, the absolute best time to plot stories.

xoxo

J.H. Croix

USA Today Bestselling Author J. H. Croix lives in a small town in the historical farmlands of Maine with her husband and two spoiled dogs. Croix writes steamy contemporary romance with sassy women and alpha men who aren't afraid to show some emotion. Her love for quirky small-towns and the characters that inhabit them shines through in her writing. Take a walk on the wild side of romance with her bestselling novels!

Places you can find me:
jhcroixauthor.com
jhcroix@jhcroix.com